On That Starry Night

On That Starry Night
Copyright © 2021 Linda Fields
All Rights Reserved
Ver 1.0
Editor: Lorilyn Roberts
Cover Designer: Lisa Vento
Interior Designer: Steven Plummer
Images: Marty Jones

Religion/Devotional
First Edition

Scripture quotations marked (NIV) are taken from the Holy Bible, New International Version®, NIV®. Copyright © 1973, 1978, 1984, 2011 by Biblica, Inc.™ Used by permission of Zondervan. All rights reserved worldwide. www.zondervan.com. The "NIV" and "New International Version" are trademarks registered in the United States Patent and Trademark Office by Biblica, Inc.™

No part of this book may be reproduced or utilized in any form or by any means, graphics, electronic or mechanical, or by any information storage and retrieval system, or used in any manner without the prior written permission of the copyright owner, except for the use of brief quotations in a book review.

Because of the ever-changing nature of the Internet, web addresses and/or links contained in this book may have changed since publication and may no longer be valid.

ISBN 13 Hardcover: 978-1-7353927-0-7
ISBN 13 Paperback: 978-1-7353927-1-4
ISBN 13 E-book: 978-1-7353927-2-1

Library of Congress Number: 2020912438

Printed in the United States of America

Acknowledgment of Praise

Lorilyn Roberts, award-winning Christian author of the *Seventh Dimension Series*, rescued my "infinity" book. She authored other books, including her newly released *Tails and Purrs for the Heart and Soul*. As a day job, Lorilyn works as a closed-captioned editor for television. Her other adventures include nurturing relationships with her two adopted daughters, public speaking, and writer workshops. She is President of the Gainesville Chapter of Word Weavers International and founder of the John 3:16 Marketing Network.

How did she find the time to polish a book that was under construction for 30 years? First, Lorilyn has a discerning sense of the voice of God in her life. She was obedient to Him in attending an Understanding the Times Conference in Minneapolis in September 2019. God used her obedience in ways she, nor I could have orchestrated.

The manuscript began when my kids were young. I worked on it through the years, but the thought of finishing the work the Lord led me to write was a battle. However, the Holy Spirit would not be hushed and continued to prompt me. Early one morning, the Lord whispered, "You need to complete what I have begun." Out of exasperation and shock, I audibly heard my voice say, "Lord, I do not care if the book is published. My children and siblings will have it. Other than that, I do not care if it goes any further. If you want it published, you are going to have to drop someone into my lap that can give me direction, and usually, you do not do that kind of thing!" Two weeks later, while flying from Minneapolis to Florida, the Lord surprised me by dropping Lorilyn into the plane seat (almost in my lap) beside me. The divine arranged meeting was the beginning of her ministry in my life.

Second, Lorilyn has a heart for the Lord and a passion for speaking His truth through writing. She enthusiastically motivated and directed me through completing the manuscript when she heard I was traveling a journey of composition that seemed unending. Her schedule was hectic and filled with prior commitments. Lorilyn took the time to refine *On That Starry Night*. She sacrificially and unselfishly became my mentor, counselor, editor, and encourager. Lorilyn, it is with the deepest gratitude, love, and respect that I thank you for the talent, timeless hours, and God-directed words of encouragement that flowed from your heart and brought the completion of this work. I daily praise and thank the Lord for the grace gift of knowing you and the impact you have had on me and my walk with Jesus, the Baby of Bethlehem. Thank you, my dear lovely friend.

In the same way, Lorilyn polished my book Pam Rasmussen buffed it. Her analytical mind allowed her to see every sentence that did not have a period, words that needed capitalization, thoughts that begged clarification, and the silly mistakes that had been passed over by others and myself. Pam, we have worked together on various projects and events over the past twenty years. You were a blessing as we planned, struggled, and laughed together, bringing them to completion. In the same way, you remained constant through long hours, late nights, and early mornings as you worked on my book. Your wit, wisdom, knowledge of God's word, gentle spirit, and love for Christ were the light that kept burning. Thank you, my cherished friend and dear Sister-in-Christ.

Thank you, Melody Chapman, my talented sister, for sharing the memories of A Decorated Box. The words remind us that our Lord uses the simple things of life and humble hearts to shine light into darkness.

Thank you, Fran Yeager, for being the prayer power behind this project. The card you sent me with the words, "Believe He can through you!" sets on my desk as a constant reminder that success comes at the hand of Jesus.

Thank you, Debi Carlson, for your wit, encouraging words, and honest critiquing of my work. Your continual interest, suggestions, prayers, and friendship have been of utmost value and have made the book more than it would have been without your keen insight and Godly wisdom.

Steven Plummer, your interior design has moved the manuscript to a higher level. The images and artwork are exquisite. Thank you for enhancing my book with your creative talents.

Lisa Vento, your creative talents produced a book cover that speaks precisely of the message within its pages. Thank you for your honesty and insight that made it possible for my mind to look beyond my thoughts and ideas to something far more beautiful than I could have ever imagined.

Thank you, Marilyn Pingue, Patti Daniels and Christie Woods, for taking the time from your busy schedules to read and critique *On That Starry Night*. Your suggestions and comments were taken seriously and pushed the manuscript closer to clarity and professionalism.

Thank you, Marty Jones, for coming to my rescue by creating the images of The Prophet and The Victorious King. They are perfect.

On That Starry Night

AN ADVENT DEVOTIONAL

LINDA FIELDS

TABLE OF CONTENTS

Introduction 15

Love's Embrace 19

Symbolism of the Advent Wreath 23

Devotional One: A Predicted Birth 27
    O Come Thou Long Expected Jesus 29
    Dad Promised 31
    Anticipation 34
    The Old One 37
    My Story 39

Devotional Two: A Holy Birth 41
    O, Holy Night 43
    Treasures of the Snow 45
    The Face of God 47
    A Christmas Wonder 51
    My Story 53

Devotional Three: A Beneficial Birth 55
    Silent Night 57
    Just One Drop 60

Written in Red	61
A Decorated Box	65
My Story	69

Devotional Four: A Lowly Birth 71
O, Little Town of Bethlehem	73
"Behold, The Lamb of God!"	74
Lamb of Hope	78
The Christmas Window	81
My Story	84

Devotional Five: A Royal Birth 85
Joy to the World	87
A Lion's Cub	89
The Lion's Roar	91
Birth of the King	95

Afterword 99
History of the Advent 103
References 107

ENDORSEMENT

I first met Linda Fields and her husband, Don, when I served as a professor at Calvary Bible College in Kansas City, MO. Even then, Linda demonstrated leadership qualities serving with the Student Wives Fellowship Organization at the college with my wife, Delores. Both Linda and Don have been faithful friends of my present ministry as well as lifetime associates and friends.

Linda has and continues to serve effectively as a pastor's wife, a successful parent, and an outstanding Christian woman. Her present skill as an author will speak for itself once readers enjoy her storytelling method. She writes with an understanding of Scripture plus passion so often absent in Christian writing. Her book is easy to read and adaptable for family devotions and educating young children in the history of Christmas and the biblical narrative as it relates to the Advent Season.

I highly recommend this work of love and trust our Lord will use it for His glory.

Dr. James B. Raiford
Founder and teacher
James B. Raiford Ministries Inc.
Author of The Camouflaged Church

DEDICATION

To My Husband, Don Fields

Don has committed his life to standing firm on the truths of Scripture. He has faithfully taught the Word of God to our four children by living an uncompromised life of grace and unconditional love. His integrity and sweet humility as a shepherd-servant pastor models Christ. His passion for Truth imparts eternal value into the hearts to whom he ministers.

Our children and spouses have consistently encouraged and supported this journey of mine. John (son) and Missy, Lacy (daughter) and Chip, Jason (son) and Monica, and Jeremy (son) and Meg have followed in Don's footprints as they stand for Truth. My heart is full of gratitude as they pass God's solid and absolute truth on to our grandchildren.

AUTHOR'S NOTE

Stories of memories in this book are from my childhood. My intent is to present them as truthfully and faithfully as possible.

INTRODUCTION

No time of the year so loudly summons humankind to reminisce and bring forth tradition as the Christmas season. From ages past to present, the days and weeks leading up to Christmas bring sweet memories to our hearts and minds—memories made in childhood and birthed in tradition.

The hustle and bustle of Christmas baking, Christmas shopping, and gathering with those whom we love create excitement and joy. Yet, amid the celebration, in the flicker of a moment, a profound awakening takes place, alerting man's heart to a bit of wonderment and questioning where and why the tradition of celebrating Christmas had its origin.

One should fear not only the glamour and pomp overshadowing the Christmas season but also the resentment and disdain that darkens long-held cultural traditions. Spiritual absolutes and principles are being challenged and compromised as believers become afraid or embarrassed to fight the Christmas war.

We falter and timidly refuse to speak as judges ban nativity scenes from public places, and school children are no longer allowed to sing Christmas carols that mention the name of Jesus. Churches are abandoning Christmas pageants, cantatas, and Christmas Eve candle-light services that not many years ago were recognized as acts of worship to the new-born King.

Embracing this concern motivated our family to pursue a tradition established long ago—THE ADVENT.

The problem of embracing the tradition was the simplicity of an Advent wreath and the absence of written material that could be used as a guide through the Advent. There were no books in the marketplace that fit the aspirations we desired. So, out of urgency, *On That Starry Night* took form.

This book is unique. Christmas devotionals sold today concentrate on the birth of Jesus. They are designed with motivational readings to get us through the holidays. They tell us how to be blessed, strengthened, and uplifted. They tell us the real meaning of Christmas. Some tell stories from Christmas characters like Mary, Joseph, the innkeeper, and shepherds. The ones we take to heart are the stories of how lives have been changed by the touch of Jesus. I am not critical. They are good and exceptional devotionals. They have purpose and intent. They motivate us to look beyond the struggles of the day and direct us to the birth of Jesus in the stable in Bethlehem. However, they miss the mark. Christmas is about a person, not an event.

On That Starry Night steps out of the norm. It is exclusive. Instead of focusing on the event of Jesus's birth, it draws us to the Person of Jesus. One extraordinary aspect of the book includes histories of Christmas carols, introducing each author, the event which prompted its writing, and why they were written. Other elements include five devotionals identifying divine attributes of Jesus, exploring His names and their meanings, and personal stories, making Christmas so memorable for me.

While writing the book, I began to grasp the significance of Advent and realized there must be a profound longing in the heart of men and women calling for a richer, fuller knowledge of the person we call Jesus. Who is He? What part did He play in the formation of the first Christmas Day? What was His purpose in life? Why does His name carry a legacy that has withstood the changing philosophy of time? *On That Starry Night* answers those questions. The book defines why the name of Jesus stands above all other names in a culture waging war against THAT name and the Christ of Christmas. It focuses on Immanuel in unobstructed clarity.

The names of Jesus throughout Scripture describe His union with God and speak of His divine nature. Understanding His names should draw us into a closer relationship with Him. The attributes of Jesus are not generally associated with baby Jesus but are attributed to Him as an adult. However, what Jesus was as a baby, and still is, was given to Him long before He entered the world. Jesus is God. He is eternal and is all that the Father is in holiness, love, and justice.

Names provided in the devotionals are: The Anointed One, Immanuel—God with us, Jesus-Savior, Lamb of God, King—The Lion of Judah.

Aspects of the birth of Christ are alive. His birth was a Predicted Birth, a Holy Birth, a Beneficial Birth, a Lowly Birth, and a Royal Birth.

Completion of the devotionals was the beginning of the journey. The next trek took me to new discoveries. I walked through centuries, looked through windows of the past, and was introduced to amazing people. The road led me to a unique and rare feature that was added to the book: CHRISTMAS CAROLS.

> My prayer and purpose is for you to become knowledgeable of their impact on history.
>
>

Christmas music echoed throughout the rooms of our small house as my mother played her holiday albums on a worn turntable. On Thanksgiving night, the voices of Frank Sinatra, Burl Ives, Andy Williams, and so many others became a hint that Christmas was on its way. At an early age, my heart embraced the splendor of each melody and lyric. Even now, my heart yearns to hear carols long before the holidays are upon us. Could I disregard the love I have for the songs and not make them a part of this book? No.

My prayer and purpose are for you to become knowledgeable of their impact on history. Christmas carols have lived in the hearts of men, women, and children since that first Christmas. As years faded, shepherds undoubtedly remembered the angels praising God from the heavens. The memory of the event may have raced through the innkeeper's mind as he cleaned the cattle stall and wondered how the young mother survived the harsh conditions of the stable. The words of Mary's song to Elizabeth, "My soul doth magnify the Lord" (Luke 1:46) would certainly have played over and over in her mind.

The words are not fairytales of a white-bearded, old man sweeping the night sky with sleigh bells ringing. They are music given as a divine gift God has used throughout the ages to impact millions. They are song stories written by men and women expressing how the birth of Jesus filled their hearts and souls.

Your family will learn about exceptional carols, their authors, and composers through their rich history. The song stories are filled with beautiful and wonderful lyrics proclaiming the glory of the incarnate Christ.

As each aspect of Christ's birth unfolded and flowed over blank lines, memories of my childhood began to awaken. Tears of joy, laughter, and sadness smudged the ink as memories became written stories. They brought fondness and warmth that lingering memories often carry. These stories are at the end of each devotional. If preserving memories is a passion of yours, write them on the "MY STORY" page you will find at the end of each weekly devotional.

Once the book was written, I realized the traditional wreath our family used no longer worked. The purple candles were replaced with candle colors that reflect the attributes of Jesus. A focal point was added to separate the first candle from the last. The design reflected the essence of the Christ Child and His purpose in life. The creation of a unique wreath emerged.

The Advent wreath frames the season. It is an integral part of celebrating as it acts as a visual representing the precepts brought forth in the book. Guidance on using the wreath is provided in the section, "Symbolism of The Advent Wreath." The book and wreath are to be used together, one complementing the other.

This book envelops ancient truths through music, biblical readings, and personal stories that bring Christmas back to the family and church. They are precepts Christians cannot ignore or compromise and expect all to be well with their soul.

Embrace the truth of God's Word with your children, grandchildren, family, and friends. Welcome them with boldness unashamedly. Then listen. Listen carefully to those truths and let them settle your spirit and empower you to live the holiday season with purpose and significance. The goal is to call the heart to silence and reflect on Immanuel. The importance is an eternal focus that will direct you to be concerned about people living in darkness so that they might see the shining light in this crooked and perverse culture, which is brimming with broken hearts, pain, and damaged emotions. Hopelessness is the deafening norm. People need to hear the truth that offers hope because Immanuel is with us.

My passion is for you to embrace the wonder and glory of the reality of Jesus' birth. Allow it to transform your mind and spirit and bring His peace into your life during the Christmas season as you share it with those you love.

LOVE'S EMBRACE

CHRISTMAS IS COMING! Cool, autumn breezes and falling leaves draw our thoughts to December 25th. Christmas wreaths hang from hooks on display racks in craft stores and gift boutiques. The newest dazzling tree ornaments stunningly align shelves, and the hottest toys of the year are crowding store aisles. The Christmas season is loved, and the heart yearns for its return. It is exciting and fun. Regardless of how we choose to celebrate, it is something we embrace with enthusiasm and anticipation. It is also a time that can cause a great deal of stress, sadness, and frustration.

When our children were young, my husband pastored modest churches with low membership. We experienced the excitement of God's loving embrace as people entered new relationships with Jesus, and Satan's bondage was broken, setting them free to live guiltless days of peace and joy. But, pastors and their wives have struggles just like you. The lack of time, energy, and finances hit hard, especially during the Christmas holidays.

For the first few years of ministry, I felt downhearted as the holidays approached. Christmas plays and teas dominated my time and zapped my energy. Miles separated us from family, and limited finances made the hope of living the "Christmas dream" seem unjust and selfish of a

God who owns everything and needs nothing. Selfishness flooded my heart, causing me to dread the Christmas season rather than celebrating it as a holy day of divine worship.

Instead of rejoicing in what the Lord had graciously given, I became disheartened. My heart told me our children missed out on the joys of childhood because the gifts under their Christmas tree were not like gifts other children received on Christmas morning. Although our children were excited and satisfied with their presents, self-pity captured my mind while anger bound my heart. My emotions were uncertain as darkness shattered the wonderment and glory of the miraculous conception and virgin birth.

Year after year, I struggled to focus on the Person of Jesus. My heart pursued the temporal and barren ideology of commercialism. The daily shadow of my elusive dream was as cold as the north wind. The danger of engaging in defeating thoughts drove me to beseech the Lord concerning my attitude.

> His power washed through my heart and soul and began to transform my mind.

The Lord surprises us when we diligently pray. The Holy Spirit convicted me, making me keenly aware of my self-destructing pattern of thinking. His power washed through my heart and soul and began to transform my mind. I began to petition the Lord to give my husband and me the wisdom and knowledge to instill the richness, depth, and eternal purpose of Christmas into our children's lives.

As spring and summer of 1982 gracefully danced out of sight, the Lord poured into my heart a renewed hope. Ideas began to invade my mind. As crisp fall days faded into winter, the ideas started to take shape leading me to reflect on the warmth of my married sister's home.

After my parents died at an early age, my sister and her husband sweetly opened their home to me, my siblings, our spouses, and children. The first year we visited them during the holidays, they enriched the Christmas season by introducing the traditional German Advent.

My brother-in-law's family was German Lutheran. Advent, unlike our chaotic childhood Christmases, was a part of his heritage.

On Christmas Eve, as my brother-in-law lit the logs in the brick fireplace, our family gathered in the living room. The excitement of baking with sisters, wrapping last-minute gifts, and racing to the door as our two military brothers walked through, began to quiet. Picking up his

Bible, my brother-in-law read the events of the first Christmas from Luke 2. The night was truly a celebration of the birth of Jesus as we praised and glorified God.

Memories of Christmas Eve at my sister's house brought life to the path the Lord was clearing for me. Thanksgiving came and went. The first Sunday after Thanksgiving, I set a simple wire Advent wreath on a wooden antique tea table fringed with a scalloped top. Four purple candles and one pink nestled in the evergreen. My husband gathered our four small children into the decorated living room, where Christmas lights cast a soft glow across the floor. Our oldest son lit a purple candle. My husband read from Isaiah 9:6 (NIV), "For to us a child is born, to us, a son is given...." A prayer of gratitude flowed from our hearts. Heaven opened, rescuing our minds from the realm and care of the day, and directed us to the birth and purpose of Jesus.

The stress of finances, negative thoughts, and the hustle and bustle of Christmas faded. The sacrifice our Lord made for us became remarkably clear. An unshakable heart transformation took place within me as the presence of a Holy God filled my heart and destroyed my selfish desires. The cold northern night ended with the aroma of freshly popped corn, hot chocolate, and the precious moments we had with our children.

After two or three years of using the traditional German Advent wreath, thoughts of the immeasurable significance the celebration of Christmas encompassed caused me to realize there was considerably more to offer our children. The mystery of Jesus began with His conception, not His birth, but I had not been introduced to the profound elements of that miraculous event until I was an adult.

As a child, books, stories from the Bible, and Christmas pageants filled my Christmases with wonders of the birth of Jesus. Words of love—tender and sweet, and words I did not understand—swept through my mind each year. Words and phrases like "*Quirinius*," "found to be with child through the Holy Spirit," and "virgin birth" are not meaningful in a child's mind.

As a teenager, I embraced the love of God sending His Son to Earth but walked through those years untouched by the promised "God with us." I wanted to instill in the hearts and minds of my children the reality that the birth of Jesus was about a person, not an event.

I pondered the hidden aspects of Christ's birth. What in it revealed the Person of Jesus and His reason for becoming a man? The sweet story of shepherds, angels, a rare star, and a baby lying in a manger surrounded by sheep, cows, and horses create feelings of nostalgia. Was the written account only that, or did it convey a more profound message? Shouldn't the truths of the awesome miracle that took place at the baby's conception and birth be imparted in the hearts of generations to come? Or should the story be allowed to quietly fade from our hearts and be replaced with luster and lights?

The story has not faded, not in our family. Our children learned about Jesus from an early age. Memories of Advent still resonate in their hearts as adults. The four of them and their spouses engage their families in celebrating the Advent Season with a wreath and devotionals. Each family celebrates Advent in its own way, but all hold to the truth learned as children.

For over twenty-five years, family, friends, and church members have been invited into our home to celebrate Advent with us. They walk away from the evening knowing they have been in the presence of a Holy God. With renewed purpose and changed hearts, they look to the holidays with peace and joy. Words of encouragement from our guests, and the persistence of my children, resulted in the printing of these pages.

It is now in your hands. You have the convenience and capability of sharing *On That Starry Night* with your children, family, and friends. The eternal benefits of taking moments out of the Christmas season to focus on the reality and importance of Jesus are boundless. The trivial fades. Truth strengthens the heart. Perhaps those you love will experience the Christmas holidays with renewed purpose by finding the eternal significance of peace and grace in the Person of Jesus.

SYMBOLISM OF THE ADVENT WREATH

THE SYMBOLISM OF the traditional Advent wreath is significant. We're reminded of God's eternal nature. We're also reminded of repentance offered through the baby of Bethlehem, Jesus Christ, who will be returning to Earth again someday soon.

The traditional Advent wreath made of evergreen or holly branches forms a circle signifying there is an Everlasting Father who is the giver of life. Arranged within the wreath are five candles. Four of the candles are purple, and one is pink. One purple candle is to be lit the first Sunday of Advent with the lighting of additional candles on each of the following Sundays. Purple represents repentance and man's need to see himself as separated from a Holy God. The pink candle, lit on Christmas Eve or Christmas Day, expresses the humility of Christ.

A red or blue candle can stand in place of the pink candle. Red symbolizes the Savior who shed His blood on Calvary's Cross as an offering for sinful man and rose three days later victorious over sin, death, and hell. Blue expresses hope in an everlasting Father.

Finally, blazing light springing forth from the candles emphasizes Christ as the light in a darkened world.

The design of the traditional wreath holds no other significance. It does not encompass the essence of the Christ Child or His purpose in life. Our family wanted a unique wreath that focused on Jesus. Something surprising emerged.

We used a circular evergreen wreath that can be purchased at any craft store. Our wreath holds five candles; however, they are not the traditional purple and pink colors. Colors of the candles are suggested in this book and represent the characteristics of Jesus. They correspond with the themes of the five devotionals.

Although our first wreath was circular and made of evergreen, one of our sons and his wife created their own unique candleholder instead of a wreath. While hiking through the forest, they found a small log (approximately 6" in diameter x 18" in length) on a mountain in Oregon. The center of the log is like a hilltop rising above the grasslands. The log slopes on either side resting on a barnwood table.

After gingerly cleaning it, they carved holes in the top of the log, one for each day (30 candles) beginning on the first Sunday after Thanksgiving until Christmas Day. The candles are white, except for the five-colored candles placed strategically on the log—one for each Sunday of the Advent. If they choose, there is space to add fresh holly berries or other decorations.

Light from the candles reflects on melting wax with stunning hues. The candleholder is charming and reflects our son and his family's love for the woods and nature.

His twin brother and wife's wreath hold a Willow Tree shepherd and lamb figurine as though they stand watch like sentinels ready to protect the baby at the first sign of discomfort. Vintage ornaments and rustic decorations of birch bark and red burlap birds highlight the wreath with the nostalgia of years spent in Alaska.

The wreath our daughter's family uses has pewter candleholders that my husband and I received as a wedding gift. It was a blessing to relinquish a family heirloom to our precious daughter. Our oldest son and wife's wreath have a white Lenox dove as a centerpiece, which characterizes the spirit of hospitality they demonstrate as they open their home to others. Each family has a unique wreath. Your family might want to think about designing a wreath that mirrors its unique personality. What fun that would be as you build memories with your children.

Advent begins on the first Sunday evening after Thanksgiving. If Sundays are not convenient, plan for another night. The candle(s) should be lit before the readings. On the first night, light the green candle; on the second night, light the green candle and the white candle. Each week begin a new devotional and light the candle that corresponds with that week's reading. By following this pattern throughout the season, you will be organized and focused.

Devotional One: The green candle is the eternity candle which speaks of Christ's timelessness.
Devotoional Two: The white candle stands for the holiness of Christ.
Devotional Three: The red candle expresses the precious blood of Jesus shed on the Cross of Calvary.
Devotional Four: The pink candle reflects the humility of Jesus.
Christmas Eve or Christmas Day: The purple candle reminds us that Jesus is the coming King.

Once candle(s) are lit, begin the night by reading the history of the Christmas carol followed by the devotional. The last reading is a story from my childhood. Include a time of prayer as a family. Food takes us to our comfort zone and generates laughter. Take your time; do not rush through the evening. Allow your kids to make comments and ask questions. If the devotional readings are too long for your little ones, read only the second part of the devotional and add to it as they mature.

The challenging part of the evening will be authoring your own stories. Parents can write about their childhood Christmases while sharing their stories with the children. Children, especially teenagers, are great storytellers. Let them be a part of the storytelling or, even better, challenge them to write their own Christmas story.

Right about now, you might be thinking that life is so busy and hectic during Christmas that you do not see any way to fit another activity into your week. Embracing the tradition of Advent must be intentional and purposeful. Define your purpose. Is it important enough to lay other activities aside and take one hour out of your week to instill the precious treasures of Jesus' life into the hearts and minds of your children?

Is it important enough to invite a friend or family into your home who does not know Christ as their Savior? If you honestly answered "Yes" to those questions, then you must be intentional.

You do not need to put a lot of time or effort into planning. I have done the work for you. All you need is this book, your spouse, children, a store-bought snack, a lighter for lighting candles, and a pencil for writing your memories. If you have children but do not have a spouse, the Lord will bless your efforts as you build into their lives beliefs that will hold and strengthen them through difficult times. If you do not have children, invite children of family and friends into your home. They will love it.

Plans you approach the evenings with are not essential. What is important is that you remember your purpose and intentionally allow the Lord to fill your heart with His wonder.

on That Starry Night

DEVOTIONAL ONE

A PREDICTED BIRTH

THE ANTICIPATION OF something planned, promised, and predicted is the focus of the first week of Advent. The green candle is a reminder of the Christ-child, the Alpha and the Omega, the beginning, and the end. The name Christ means "Anointed One." Old Testament prophesies identify the baby of Bethlehem by revealing Christ's divine appointment as He steps into the lives of His created ones.

The Christmas carol "O, Come Thou Long-Expected Jesus" was written with anticipation at the coming of Christ. The man who wrote the carol awoke to the realization that Jesus had come, and he had almost missed Him.

"The Old One" is the story of an old man and his wife stepping out and loving my family and our church family while making Christmas a little more exciting and meaningful.

O, Come Thou Long Expected Jesus

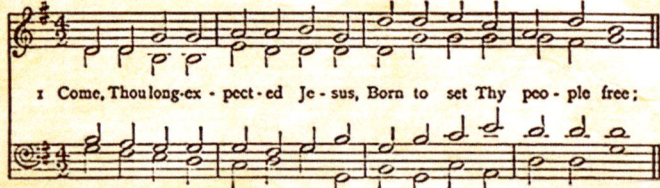

2 Israel's strength and consolation,
   Hope of all the earth Thou art;
Dear desire of every nation,
   Joy of every longing heart.

3 Born Thy people to deliver,
   Born a child, and yet a King,
Born to reign in us for ever,
   Now Thy gracious kingdom bring.

4 By Thine own eternal Spirit,
   Rule in all our hearts alone:
By Thine all-sufficient merit,
   Raise us to Thy glorious throne. Amen.

DEVOTIONAL ONE: A PREDICTED BIRTH

O, Come Thou Long Expected Jesus
Charles Wesley
12-18-1707-03/29/1788
Year: 1744
Composer: John Frederick Lampe
Year: 1746

I, Charles Wesley, following an extended trip to the New World (America), scribed a poem, "O, Come, Thou Long-Expected Jesus."

After returning from the New World, alarming concerns of my beloved England led me to extreme anguish. First was the situation with the orphans. The number of abandoned children was staggering. They had no beds, no food, and no one to protect them. Lice infected their spindly, weak bodies that reeked. The image cemented in my head. The smell, stuck in my nostrils, was pathetic and disturbing. I became nauseous and utterly unable to focus because of these little ones' overwhelming hopelessness and the inability to rescue them from destruction, abuse, and neglect.

Second was the widening class divide taking place in England. Commerce was rising, and people moved from the rural areas into London, where consumerism was the newfound hobby. As the economy increased, so did the power of politics and religion. Wealthy landlords dominated the middle class as the divide became wider. Ordinary citizens became increasingly poorer and less influential.

Third, the practice and severity of slavery had become an abomination to our Lord. Men, women, and children were being sold into slavery, defiling the principles of a loving God who created them in His own image.

From birth, I was never in the best of health. The emotional toll England's political, financial, and spiritual condition took on me led to severe physical problems and depression. Deceived by my intelligence, position, and education, I was blinded to the fact that I had a spiritual problem.

I came to realize the healing process included not only my mind and body but my soul as well. I trusted my knowledge of Scripture and work for Christ, and His Church, for my salvation.

Conversations with my Moravian friends resulted in a transformation of my heart. My weary body and fragile mind began to heal as I realized working for God did not satisfy His wrath for the sinful nature with which I was born. My works were not pleasing to God. The enlightenment that Jesus's blood, shed on the cross as the only acceptable means of salvation, flooded my heart and renewed my mind.

> I asked Jesus to forgive my sin and bring salvation to my soul. I was overwhelmed with God's grace and love for me.

Although the great class divide in England was troubling, I realized the greatest divide of all was the separation between Jesus and myself. On May 21, 1738, I asked Jesus to forgive my sin and bring salvation to my soul. I was overwhelmed with God's grace and love for me.

In 1744, while reading the prediction written by Israel's prophet, Haggai, God's Word pierced my soul. Haggai wrote, "'I will shake all nations, and what is desired by all nations will come, and I will fill this house with glory,' says the LORD Almighty" (Haggai 2:7).

My magnificent God formulated the words of the poem in my mind as I contemplated His great goodness and love for mankind and His promise to come in exceeding glory and immense power to end this world system. I penned the words around the second coming of Christ and invited God to come and dwell among us and put an end to evil as He reigned as King. My heart was renewed by the Spirit of the Living God.

However, dark conditions in this world led me to long for the One who is desired by all nations—the One who would restore His glory to this Earth.

Not only was my heart transformed, but so was my preaching. I realized my first responsibility was to teach and preach this glory from God's Word to miserable and lost sinners. My message was that of Haggai's. It was constant; yet, given at a different time, in a different place, and to different people. Their heart condition remained as their forefathers'. They, too, were broken, miserable, lost sinners. These truths burned in their ears as they recognized their hopeless, sinful state. More people than I could imagine responded to the reality of a great salvation offered only through the predicted One.

The words of the poem soon took the form of a Christmas carol that has been sung through four centuries. It draws our hearts to the fulfilled prediction of a Savior and promises the hope of the coming of the King who one day soon will establish His eternal kingdom. His was a PREDICTED BIRTH.

DEVOTIONAL

DAD PROMISED

"A promise is a promise." Logan's dad winked.

Logan felt a pounding in his chest as his dad turned with long strides and walked away. His tall, athletic body reflected the honor and dignity the army-green uniform demanded.

Logon wished he could run and give his father one last hug before the door slammed and shut on the sparkling blue Southwest airplane that was flying him to Fort Bragg. From there, he would be deployed to Iraq. It would be twelve months before Logan would see him again.

The memory of that day played in Logan's head far too often. He remembered precisely what his father had promised: A trip to Disney World for his tenth birthday, just the two of them.

Logan counted as the days, weeks, and months slowly passed. Eleven months were marked on his calendar. His dad had just called from a satellite phone at the Army base. He thought he heard the words, "I may not be home for your birthday, Son. I might have to stay in Iraq longer than…" A fuzzy, crackling sound came over the phone and then dead silence.

"A promise is a promise," echoed in Logan's head.

It would be two weeks before he could talk to his dad again. That was too long to have to wait for an explanation. His birthday was sixteen days away. His father had to make it home. He just had to. He promised.

Logan had lived through this before. He remembered his father being deployed for eighteen months and not able to return when scheduled. His stomach ached as the disappointment returned. Logan thought about his dad's promise and the odds that he would be able to keep it.

Uncle David banged twice and shoved the oak door open as he dashed into the living room. He was young, single, and always ready for an adventure.

"Hi, Uncle David," Logan shouted, happy to see him.

Uncle David reached over and scuffed Logan's hair. "Hey, don't you have a birthday coming up real soon?"

"Yep!" moaned Logan.

"Well, you don't have to be so happy about it," Uncle David teased. "What's going on? You should be excited."

"Before Dad left for Iraq, he promised me he would be home for my birthday and take me to Disney World. It was going to be an awesome time just for us, father and son. Dad said so, and now he might not be able to come home."

"Hmm!" Uncle David breathed deeply. "What about this? If your father does not make it home for your birthday, I predict that I will take you to Disney World."

Logan was excited. "Wow! Really? That would be great, Uncle David." Logan thought a second, frowned, and asked, "What do you mean, you predict? Can't you promise, like my dad?"

"If I promise, I might not be able to keep that promise, but I predict there is a 99.9 percent chance I can take you to Disney World on your tenth birthday," offered Uncle David.

"Thanks, Uncle David! That will be a lot of fun if you and I can go." Logan smiled.

Time slowly passed. It was five days before Logan's birthday, and his dad had not come home. The youngster was discouraged, and he gave up on the thought that his father would be able to take him to Disney World. At the same time, he hoped his uncle would come through with his prediction.

As Logan tried to sleep that night, his mind churned from excitement to disappointment. He knew he had to be content with a 99.9 percent possibility that Uncle David would be standing in for his dad. His heart ached. He could not hold back the tears that for days had been wrestling to get out.

He dreamed his father was playing basketball with him and said, "A promise is a promise, Son." He roused and tried to focus his eyes in the dark. A faint light coming from a crack in the bedroom door cast the shadow of a man.

A deep voice whispered, "A promise is a promise, Son."

Logan bounded out of bed into the strong, protective arms of his father.

The two hugged each other. "We're going to Disney World for your tenth birthday, Logan, just the two of us—father and son."

In unison, their voices echoed, "A promise is a promise!"

Uncle David had picked Logan's dad up at the airport. He peeked around the bedroom door to witness the surprised expression on Logan's face when he saw his father. In a whispered, sheepish voice Uncle David asked, "Can I go, too?"

The story of Logan, his dad, and Uncle David sets the framework for distinguishing between the words "predict" and "prophecy." They are often used interchangeably. However, according to the Merriam-Webster Dictionary, to predict means to declare in advance based on observation, experience, or scientific reason, while to prophesy is an inspired utterance by a prophet regarding something to come that is of divine will and purpose. Anyone can predict; only the Spirit of Jehovah, the Revealer, can prophesy. A prediction may or may not take place. A prophecy is a promise that cannot be broken.

In the Old Testament, God insisted that a prophet must be 100 percent accurate 100 percent of the time; 99.9 percent accuracy did not work. The probability of a mistake did not exist. God can predict and prophesy with 100 percent accuracy because He is 100 percent all-knowing and all-powerful. He makes His plans succeed. He planned, promised, and predicted the person of Jesus.

Prophecies point to the timelessness of God and His eternal plan for the people He created. He existed before time and space. He WAS before the great rebellion when Lucifer fought for the throne of God. He WAS before the creation of the sun, moon, and stars. He WAS before Adam and Eve walked and talked with Him in the cool of the evening. He is eternal and knows all. In heaven's Kingdom, God knew man would need an escape from his own destruction, so He *planned* for a Redeemer.

Prophecies are a reminder of God's unfolding *promise* of redemption, weaving a beautiful tapestry of his eternal love in rescuing men from their broken and rebellious hearts and the forces of evil. He observed Adam and Eve's rejection of His love in the Garden of Eden and grieved their darkened hearts. He declared, "The man has now become like one of Us, knowing good and evil...." (Genesis 3:22). God's holiness demanded that man's sin needed to be remedied. Wickedness had now separated them from their Creator. God's grace would be the only means by which they could be reunited with Him.

Prophecies call the heart and mind to the reality that God released the first news briefing. He

> Prophecies call the heart and mind to the reality that God released the first news briefing.

✦ ✠ ✦

predicted when announcing the coming of a unique baby whose conception would be miraculous, whose first breath would be in a particular place and at the perfect time, whose life would impact man for eternity, and whose death would free men of fear and sin. Jesus is the Christ, the Anointed One, whom God introduced at the perfect time and with divine purpose.

His birth and death were planned, promised, and predicted with 100 percent accuracy.

ANTICIPATION

Excitement, waiting, and hoping are wrapped up in the days looking forward to Christmas morning. Christmas is the coming of something that is expected, something grand and something incredible. But within the excitement of its magical atmosphere, there also comes something urgently needed.

There was a time when man needed something desperately unattainable. He needed something apart from himself. He had failed. His world was dark and forlorn; hope was gone.

The man and his wife once possessed the world. They lived in great abundance and splendor. Their created minds overflowed with knowledge and wisdom, but not now. The miraculous wonders graciously given for their protection and provision vanished like vapor. Their home, food, and significance were lost; everything was gone because of one decision.

There remained nothing except defeat, depression, guilt, and shame. "If only I had listened to God!" probably echoed through the confusing thoughts that plagued their clouded, darkened minds. "If only...if only...."

Even before breath entered their bodies, there was a hint of One who cared so deeply and lovingly for them. The One, now an isolated blur, called to their wretched hearts. Fear surrounded them. Their disobedience separated them from all hope.

In the shadows of the cool evening, the One who loved them searched for them. "Adam, Eve, where are you?" Did the voice ring forth with anticipation of hope, or was all lost, forever? Would they have the chance to embrace this deep love once again?

Approximately four thousand years before Christ's birth, amid the darkest hour ever to exist, a joyful assured "sign" proclaimed a Redeemer would conquer the forces of evil. A ray of light restored hope to Adam and Eve.

The voice of Jehovah, the Revealing One, prophesied with 100 percent accuracy when he spoke to Satan, "And I will put enmity [conflict] between you and the woman, and between your offspring [demons and evil men] and hers [Christ the Redeemer]; He will crush your head [deliver you a fatal blow], and you will strike His heel [afflict the humanity of Christ]" (Genesis 3:15).

The "offspring" (seed) spoken of by the Lord refers to Satan, the ruler of the powers of this darkened world. The words "her offspring" reflect a "sign" as it gives preeminence to the Christ, born of the Virgin Mary, who one day would come to defeat the root of evil.

The Lord is recorded in Isaiah 7:14 to have given rebellious King Ahaz a sign. "Therefore, the Lord himself will give you a sign: The virgin will conceive and give birth to a son and will call him Immanuel."

Centuries later, the prediction of the Anointed One was revealed to another young man. One dark, confusing, hopeless night, Joseph heard the woman he loved so deeply declare with excitement that she was carrying a child. He knew it was not his own. In a dream, the angel of the Lord announced to this troubled carpenter that Mary remained pure. He told Joseph not to be frightened.

The messenger from God proclaimed the most powerful, supernatural act of God. "...because what is conceived in her is from the Holy Spirit.[21] She will give birth to a son, and you are to give him the name Jesus, because he will save his people from their sins" (Matthew 1:20-21). Gabriel's final word to Mary, "For nothing is impossible with God," confirmed what would be.

Hope entered the world with the incarnate Christ. From the moment the promise was given in the Garden of Eden to the announcement by Gabriel to Joseph, men and women of old had something to anticipate. They had someone to look to who was the center of all hope; someone who would redeem the world, their world, from the darkness of sin that had engulfed them.

Hope appeared in Bethlehem on the first Christmas night. Hope was wrapped in swaddling clothes and laid in a manger. In the City of David, a Savior had been born.

on That Starry Night

THE OLD ONE

A man from my childhood, Alfred, seemed as ancient as the old prophet, Isaiah. In the world's estimation, he would not have been considered a great man, nor would he have been viewed as a man of prominence or wealth in the small farming town in which I grew up. Close observers would have thought him a humble man, great only in the eyes of a child who needed a friend.

He was never dressed too grand to hold a dirty baby or too arrogant to sit at a table when the food was sparse and the menu far less than an eight-course dinner. His gentle words of wisdom and warm hugs often made the day seem a little easier to get through. He seemed to understand my dad, a gentle man, whose mind was tormented with battle scenes from Normandy during World War II as he tried to ease the pain and erase the memories with alcohol.

We often had Sunday dinner with Alfred and his wife, Leigh. Running through cornfields on their farm, after stuffing ourselves with Leigh's savory roast beef and cornbread, was the perfect place for kids to forget the troubles of the day and enjoy the sun and fresh air of country living.

The couple's rough, cracked hands told the story of years of arduous work—long days tilling acres of fields and milking herds of cows. Still, they had time and energy to love on us. That love radiated through wrinkled, smiling faces and happy embraces.

As Christmas approached each year, we excitedly anticipated seeing Alfred and Leigh. One or two days before Christmas, we would hear the rumble of an old black 1942 Chevy truck sputtering down the road and slowly turn into our driveway. Struggling to get out of the vehicle, the elderly couple delivered boxes of crisp Yellow Delicious apples and crates of juicy oranges to our front door. We danced with delight, for we did not often have such luxury.

Another fond memory of Alfred is when he stood beside the freshly cut tree that majestically adorned the front of our small-town Baptist church. His stately form reflected a once tall and strong young man full of energy and vitality as the hymnal swayed back and forth in his hand.

As he led the timid congregation in carols of praise and worship to our Lord, his body gently swayed from side to side. His hand balanced the hymnal with soft, natural, up and down gestures as his eyes filled with tears. His rough, old voice rang loud and clear above the rest, "O little town of Bethlehem, how still we see thee lie...."

When the singing and Christmas pageant brought a close to the evening of festivity, Alfred stood at the church's backdoor clutching brown paper bags brimming with Christmas candy, fruit, and nuts. Every child from age one to 99 was handed a bag of treats and wished a "Merry Christmas."

Throughout our years of ministry, I have been, and continue to be, inspired by Alfred and Leigh's gift of weaving excitement and happiness into Christmas and by the love and acceptance they demonstrated to my siblings and me. Now, I share the history of Christmas carols, write plays, direct pageants, and enjoy Christmas teas. My greatest treasure is gathering with the youth group and a couple of women from the church to fill brown paper bags with candy, fruit, nuts, and in addition a candy cane.

When the singing and Christmas pageant are over, I stand with the teens at the back of the church, where we offer brown paper bags of goodies to the congregation as they button their coats and walk out into the cold, dark night. Perhaps memories will be made and cherished in the hearts of children as we wish a "Merry Christmas" to all.

Years ago, Alfred gave up his position beside the Christmas tree. He relinquished it for something spectacular and more glorious than anything this world had to offer.

Though time has slipped away, my thoughts of Alfred leading the church choir remain. Memories intertwine with the reality of Alfred's present home. I imagine looking through heaven's window. There he stands with the redeemed, proclaiming, "Worthy is the Lamb that was slain."

Once the song fades, he rests at the feet of Jesus. With his guitar by his side, harmonica in one hand and a child on his lap, he brings to completion the song he once sang on Earth, "The hopes and fears of all the years are met in Thee tonight."

As you write your own story, think of an event or person who built moments of excitement and anticipation into your Christmas as a child.

DEVOTIONAL ONE: A PREDICTED BIRTH

MY STORY

DATE: _____
AUTHOR: _____
TITLE: _____

On That Starry Night

DEVOTIONAL TWO

A HOLY BIRTH

THE NAME OF Christ, Immanuel, is the focus of the second week of Advent. Immanuel means "God with us." The soft glow of a white lit candle will be a reminder that Jesus is the perfect, Holy God who lives in our presence.

"O Holy Night" is a lovely carol with a sweet message of the night of our dear Savior's birth. It was written by a man who lived his life opposite of the treasure that slept in his heart.

Two young girls witnessed a wonder in the Christmas sky. It was unexplainable, as were the questions in their minds. In the story "A Christmas Window," you can hear the voices of the youngsters struggling for truth.

DEVOTIONAL TWO: A HOLY BIRTH

O, Holy Night
Placide Cappeau
10/25/1808-08/08/1877
Year: 1847
Composer:
Adolphe Adam
Year: 1847

Allow me to introduce myself, Placide Cappeau. My passion was quite the opposite of other "religious" songwriters. I was no preacher, nor could you refer to me as a spiritual man. No, I was a wine merchant described by clergy as "a social radical, a freethinker, a socialist and a non-Christian." Occasionally, I tried my hand at poetry. Well, one hand anyway, as I had lost the other at age eight in a firearms accident.

My home, nestled in the small town of Roquemaure, France, was a safe fortress from the ugliness of the world. Or so I thought. The parish priest was not particularly fond of me; however, he praised me for my works of poetry. This one thing motivated him to persuade me to use my talents for the Almighty rather than foolish worldly pleasures.

He needed a song for his Christmas Eve mass. His skeptical tone told me he was not confident I could conquer the task. The truth is, neither was I. Even at that, I felt honored at the invitation to share my expertise.

I was inspired to write the song on a business trip to Paris on December 3, 1847. Pulling my mother's tattered old Bible from my bag, I read the words from Luke 2. As the events captivated my mind, people and places came alive. Lyrics started to flow from heart to pen. I scribbled the words before they vanished from my thoughts.

Upon my arrival, I took the lyrics to an acquaintance and composer, Adolphe Adam. Being a man of Jewish heritage, Adolphe opposed the celebration of a mere baby for anything, much less for being called the Messiah, the Son of God. As a professional and honorable man, he dismissed his beliefs for a time and put the words to music.

I enthusiastically returned to Roquemaure and presented the song to the priest. Three weeks later, I was persuaded to attend Midnight Mass where the music was heard for the first time that Christmas Eve. The aahs and tears of parishioners told me the song had touched their hearts, and I was moved as well.

However, it was not well received by clergy in the area. They did not align with my way of thinking or living. One bishop denounced the song, declaring it "lacked musical taste and was absolutely absent of the spirit of religion." My beloved Roquemaure was no longer a place of shelter, but one of tension and isolation.

The influence of church leaders soon faded. Before Christmas of 1855, the carol had been translated into German, French, Latin, and other languages and published in England. The song made history on different occasions.

Soldiers, reportedly, sang the song on the battlefield during the Franco-Prussian War. Their performance received a standing ovation in concert halls around the world. For two centuries, churches have weaved it into Christmas pageants. The most fascinating story connects men at sea with Christmas Eve onshore.

The night was bitter, the full moon hung brilliantly in the black sky, and the wind howled as it fiercely tossed ships at sea. Crew members longed to be home for the holidays. On December 24, 1906, Reginald Fessenden, a university professor and radio broadcaster from Brant Rock, Massachusetts, did something unspeakable. For the first time in history, he used a newly developed generator and microphone to broadcast over airwaves.

Fessenden's voice was heard loud and clear through the speaker's snaps and crackles as he opened the night by reading the events surrounding the birth of Jesus. Astonished radio operators turned the knobs to get a clear message. After the reading, Fessenden played Handel's "Largo."

As the evening slipped away, the crewmen's spirits soared, their hearts filled with peace, and their minds were set free to embrace the splendor and glory of the celebration of the birth of Jesus. The sailors cherished the moments as Fessenden played "O Holy Night" on his violin.

My heart filled with joy knowing the world celebrated the night of our dear Savior's birth with a song that had been rejected by clergy. The song's words tell the story of my heart and the truths I know of the Savior's HOLY BIRTH.

DEVOTIONAL

TREASURES OF THE SNOW

The majestic elegance of an intricate snowflake swirling in the wind echoes the Holiness of God. Each storehouse of crystal reflects His purity.

Although a white candle beautifully represents the character of God, it is not pure. Wax candles are made from petroleum, contaminating them with impurities. Jesus came to Earth in holiness and purity. He has no contaminants. He is whiter than the new-fallen snow and is the only one pure enough to give Himself, through His Son, to those He loves.

Moses wrote in Job 38:22, "Have you entered the storehouses of the snow…?" When Job walked the Earth, snow was, and still is, a mysterious miracle filled with treasures.

Each unique snowflake declares God's artistic character. The human mind is finite. To comprehend the immeasurable power of God's creative intelligence is inconceivable. He is like an artist sketching each snowflake as it emerges like a stunning six-sided star reflecting light, making the translucent wonder appear white. God is not overwhelmed as He delicately weaves each line, angle, and point. As steady as a jeweler's hand, He gently layers tiny ice crystals and paints them as pictures of diamonds.

As crystals adhere to one another, a wonderland of elegance springs forth. Brown, barren tree branches glisten like crystal. Lakes and ponds sparkle as though a wave of diamonds have merged and settled above the waters. Fields of sunflowers and fireweed whither under a blanket of breathtaking loveliness. Like white wax, even the solid whiteness of the snow and its unique crystal composition are not pure.

Illustrations break down when attempting to describe the character of God. Old Testament authors tried to explain it.

They used the word "snow" to represent purity, depicting it as a contrast between black and white. In Psalm 51:7, David acknowledged his transgressions before a holy God. He pleaded for God's mercy and great compassion toward "all" his sin and the darkness which had taken residence in his soul. "Cleanse me with hyssop, and I will be clean; wash me, and I will be whiter than snow."

Isaiah 1:18 records God's voice, "…though your sins are like scarlet, they shall be as white as snow." Snow was the whitest white Old Testament writers had as a reference.

That is not the case in today's world. In 1986, scientists developed a material designed to be used in medical diagnostic equipment. The substance enhances the scattering of light.

It reflects 99 percent of the visible light that hits it. Technicians refer to the material as Spectralon—"the whitest white." It reflects a higher amount of light than anything else. The material must be free of contaminants to retain its reflective properties.

Opposite from the "whitest white" is the "blackest black." Vantablack absorbs 99.965 percent of visible light. However, in 2019, engineers created a coating used on cameras, vehicles, and other products that demand an indestructible covering. It is ten times darker than Vantablack. The absorption rate is 99.995 percent of visible light. It is so black it emerges as a black void.

God is the whitest white. He is Holy. He cannot retain His holy character if the tiniest particle of contamination penetrates His Spirit, but that is an impossibility, or He could not be God.

On the contrary, man is not pure. Isaiah 5:20 says that man views good as evil and evil as good. Not only does man not see a Holy God, neither does he see his own sinful heart. To God, sin is the blackest black. It leaves a black void in the heart of man. Black happens when there is no light.

One might ask, "Who gave God the title 'Holy'? By what right and authority is that name given Him?"

By His own authority God calls Himself Holy. His spotless character gives Him the freedom to refer to Himself as holy. Is He, then, a narcissist? No, He knows His character and is comfortable with who He is. He proclaims His holiness to "all people, for all times, for all places," as Josh McDowell wrote in his book *Right from Wrong*.

During the early years of the created world, God said to the new nation, Israel, "I am the Lord your God; consecrate yourselves and be holy, because I am holy" (Leviticus 11:44). God allowed other voices to speak of His character. The Psalmist praised God because of His justice and holiness. "Exalt the Lord our God and worship at his holy mountain; for the LORD, our God is holy" (Psalm 99:9).

Jesus confirmed God's holiness when He prayed, "Our Father who art in heaven, 'Holy' is Your name." Jesus was fearless. He made the stunning announcement that not only was His Father holy, but He was holy. In proclaiming this, He acknowledged Himself as equal with God. Jesus was unashamed to equate Himself with the Father. The supreme God released

Himself to leave the grandeur of heaven and make His journey through the blackest black world in the form of the Man, Immanuel.

When visible light hits Spectralon at the strike point of a surface, light scatters and bounces back at different angles. A canopy of brilliant light forms as the light bounces back. The blackest black absorbs visible light. Any light that hits the strike point is immediately absorbed and snuffed out.

Jesus is the luminous light from heaven. Unlike the blackest black absorbing any light that hits the strike point, the light of Jesus cannot be snuffed out.

THE FACE OF GOD

The angel, Gabriel, announced to Mary, "The Holy Spirit will come on you, and the power of the Most High will overshadow you. So the holy one to be born will be called the Son of God" (Luke 1:35).

Gabriel's insight when announcing the news to Mary does something an ultrasound cannot do. An ultrasound cannot penetrate the heart, soul, or character of a person. Gabriel knows the heart of Jesus and defines the essence of who He is. He is the Holy One, the Son born of a virgin, whom Isaiah called Immanuel, God with us. "Therefore, the Lord himself will give you a sign. The virgin will conceive and give birth to a son, and will call him Immanuel" (Isaiah 7:14).

Jesus is Holy and He is God! He is a divine living being who communicates with, cares for, and loves His creation so much that He came into the world to shop the marketplace, eat dinner with us, hold our babies, laugh and celebrate the good times, and cry with us through sad and lonely times.

That describes our dads, husbands, sons, and brothers. What made Jesus different from these men? It could not have been His development in the womb or His birth. His growth was fully human, the same as any baby.

However, the conception of Jesus was not ordinary. The event was incomprehensible, distinguishing Him from every male figure in our lives. Unlike all babies, Jesus did not have a biological father. A Holy God, through the Holy Spirit, is His Father. It had to be that way, or Jesus could not be God.

To deny the incarnation, that God became Man, is a logical and reasonable conclusion for one who does not grasp the historical and supernatural event of the conception of Christ. It is not the formation or birth of Immanuel that is disturbing to the mind of man. But instead, it is the conception through the power of the Holy Spirit that causes some people's thinking to falter, question, and even deny Christ's incarnation. "Why?" Because man cannot explain or comprehend such miraculous happenings.

Mary first asked the question that rings through the ages, "How will this be since I am a virgin?" The angel confidently and knowingly responded that the Holy Spirit and the power of the Most-High would take care of her concern.

Nowhere in Scripture is Joseph referred to as the father of Jesus. Jesus is the "offspring" of the woman. Six hundred years before Christ, the Prophet Isaiah correctly foretold that a virgin would conceive and bear a Son. Matthew's account of Gabriel's visit with Joseph states, "What is conceived in her is from the Holy Spirit." Scripture affirms Christ became the Son of Man; He was never the son of a man. A Holy God became man through the conception of the Holy Spirit.

People wonder how a Holy God can be born of a sinful woman. Some scholars answer it by declaring sin could not have stained Mary. However, Mary expressed her need for a Savior when she sang her song of praise, "My soul glorifies the Lord[47] and my spirit rejoices in God my Savior,[48] for he has been mindful of the humble state of his servant" (Luke 1:46-48).

Mary saw herself standing in the presence of a Holy God unworthy to be called anything other than a "handmaid," ready to serve her Savior.

God took the form of a baby. Psalm 139:13-16 affirms the magnificent and miraculous creation of life:

> [13]For you created my inmost being; you knit me together in my mother's womb.[14] I praise you because I am fearfully and wonderfully made; your works are wonderful, I know that full well.[15] My frame was not hidden from you when I was made in the secret place, when I was woven together in the depths of the earth. [16] Your eyes saw my unformed body; all the days ordained for me were written in your book before one of them came to be.

With His almighty power, the Creator designed the innermost being of Jesus as He has done throughout millenniums with all babies. God perfectly created Jesus in the protective comfort of His mother's womb. God attentively and purposely organized every eye, ear, finger, and toe to develop in the exact place that would bring honor and glory to Him.

As with all babies, Immanuel grew in His mother's womb for nine months. During her fourth month of pregnancy, her baby fluttered within her womb. Mary experienced discomfort and pain like all mothers. In Bethlehem's stable, she gave birth to her precious baby boy.

The first time Mary gazed upon the face of God, she must have examined His eyes, counted His fingers and toes, and touched His soft, olive-colored skin. There was no halo, only the beautiful raven-black hair of His Jewish heritage.

The creative attribute of God designed the physical frame of Immanuel to be as ordinary as any man. He could move through the crowds without being identified. He passed through cornfields with His disciples. He did not wear a purple, regal robe with a celestial halo hovering over His head. When in a fishing boat, Immanuel did not wear a long, white gown illuminating a bright, glistening light that radiated from His body. His physical anatomy was like all men. Baby Jesus is the preexistent God who made His dwelling on Earth.

When your heart asks Mary's question, "How can this be?" embrace Gabriel's answer that God's Word will never fail, and with Him, all things are possible.

As we approach Christmas, the truth "God's Word will never fail," should burn in our hearts. To deny the incarnation would be a tragedy. Our hearts should ask, "What is the purpose of this miraculous event? Why did God become Immanuel?"

There was only one purpose for God to become a man. He knew He was the only one capable of having an eternal relationship with humankind. Salvation demanded a sacrifice. Jesus is the only person who could satisfy God's plan of redemption. On the Cross of Calvary, God's justice was satisfied. Rising victorious from the tomb, Jesus displayed God's power and authority by defeating evil and the sting of death.

A mother's hope in giving birth is for her baby to live. The Holy One of Bethlehem came to die. Through His death, Christ offers to man eternal life and fulfills His Promise to be with us in the dark, deep hours of life's longest night. In our pain, tears, and turmoil His arms embrace us with everlasting love.

On That Starry Night

A CHRISTMAS WONDER

Life was simple in the tiny two-bedroom house that my eight siblings and I called home. Nothing changed from day to day. School and homework filled weekdays. Weekends set us free to explore the woods, play football in the alley between rows of houses, and stay up late playing Monopoly and eating popcorn.

The summers were epic! Hot days were filled with climbing trees, swimming in the farmer's pond, and playing baseball. My brothers were on the city hardball team, and my sisters and I were on the city softball team. When we were not playing for the city, we made our teams playing siblings against siblings.

Winter and Christmas holidays changed the dynamics of our home. The little house became alive with excitement. Snow fell softly, covering the ground with a white blanket of glistening beauty. The Christmas tree was chosen, cut, and decorated with simple ornaments that withstood the test of time as unstable hands of adolescence struggled to reach the highest point of the tree.

Each year, one or two decorations did not make it through the season, nor would the tree be standing on Christmas Eve had it not been tied with fishing wire to curtain rods. Thoughts of gifts under the tree on Christmas morning danced in our heads as we said good night.

As the years passed, excitement faded in my heart and mind as well as in my younger sister's. Santa must not have gotten our Christmas list. The neighborhood kids opened gifts of bikes and scooters, BB guns, adorable new dresses, and roller skates. Toys like that never made it to our house on Christmas morning.

We wondered, "Is there even a Santa Claus?"

On Christmas Eve, when I was seven years old and my sister was six, we took one long, last look for Santa as we stood on the bed gazing out the window with arms crossed over a scratched, dented, metal bed frame. A serious discussion about the reality of Santa Claus took our imagination into another realm.

As we watched the soft, delicate snowflakes touch the frozen ground, lights magically appeared in the night sky. Santa and his eight reindeer sailed between the stars, swooping closer to the window with each second. Our hearts pounded as we intensely watched the flying object.

Convincing each other that it was Santa and his reindeer was not a challenging task. We began to bounce and shout with glee for the younger children to "come and see."

Before the little ones made it to the window, the lights vanished just as quickly as they appeared. My sister and I were disappointed that the younger kids did not get to see Santa. We assured them Santa would be coming down the chimney as soon as the lights were out and our eyes closed in a deep sleep.

Alone once again, we pursued the discussion about Santa. Was it *really* Santa we saw or was it an airplane? Our young minds could not answer those questions. Our thoughts were full of the belief and hope that had been put there by Christmas songs, catalogs, and TV commercials coloring our childhood concept of what Christmas should be. And despite my mother's counsel, our hearts had been betrayed by a Jolly Old Man who never brought gifts that were on our Christmas list.

My mother overheard the disappointed and confused words of her little girls. As she dusted flour from her tattered and stained white apron on which printed violets fell in random form, she sat on the bedside, pulled us close, and explained the wonder of Christmas.

She whispered, "It is not wise for children to envy what others have and to believe they will enjoy the same gifts their friends receive. Happiness in life does not depend on owning the hottest toys that align store shelves, or that are advertised on T.V. or in catalogs. Contentment comes when a child is grateful for the presents they receive because they sprang from a heart of love in the givers. That love is the true miracle of Advent.

The unanswered questions began to fade from our minds. And that was okay because, with my mother's wise counsel, my sister and I concluded that celebrating Christ's birth is *not* believing there is a Santa Claus or acquiring the same trendy treasures collected by schoolmates. Rather, it is a world of awe, beauty, and holiness that springs forth from a heart in love with Jesus, the Babe of Bethlehem—God's precious gift to us.

As a child, did you have questions about Santa? What questions did you have, and how were they answered? Writing your story may help your children settle related questions in their minds. Or encourage them to write their own ideas and discuss them with your family.

DEVOTIONAL TWO: A HOLY BIRTH

MY STORY

DATE: _____

AUTHOR: _____

TITLE: _____

DEVOTIONAL THREE

A BENEFICIAL BIRTH

THE RED CANDLE is to be lit during the third week of Advent. The color speaks of the greatest gift a person can give—his own life and blood for someone who does not love him. It also symbolizes the most significant emotion a person can experience—LOVE.

This week's name is Jesus, which means Savior. Jesus was a common Jewish name, but Jesus was not a common man; He was God! His purpose in living was to die by shedding His blood on the Cross, making it possible for us to have eternal life.

One of the most cherished Christmas carols of all times draws us to the night Christ the Savior was born. "Silent Night" sprang from the heart of a man who was snatched from poverty and given gifts that changed the course of his life.

"A Decorated Box" was written by my sister. A box filled with toys and Christmas cookies secretly made it to the door of a poor family, but days later, a twist of events changed everything.

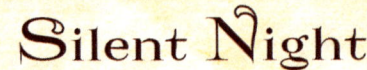

DEVOTIONAL THREE: A BENEFICIAL BIRTH

Silent Night
Josef Mohr
12/11/1972-12/04/1848
Year: 1816
Composer:
Franz Gruber
Year: 1818

My name, Josef Mohr, caused me extreme embarrassment; however, as you will soon learn, I did not allow my past to paralyze my future.

My father, Franz Mohr, was raised in Mariapfarr, Austria, and had acquired a blackened reputation. He was an unscrupulous soldier and deserter who sold his soul to the military for deceit and personal monetary gain. My mother, Anna Schoiberin, an embroiderer, birthed four children outside of marriage. I was born into poverty and knew the brokenness, hunger, and crime that engulfed Austria's dingy, poverty-stricken cities.

Miraculously, God reached down into my shattered life and liberated me from the stench of the city and sin-stricken behavior I could have embraced. I sensed God's imprint on my life. Along with angels, my heart sang "Alleluia" and "Praise" to our King for the acts of grace He gifted to me.

Vicar Johann Nepomuk Hiernle, a Benedictine monk, recognized my musical talents and introduced me to a new world. He took me under his wing and instilled in me a servant's heart as I sang and played the violin in the choir at the University Church and the Monastery of St. Peter. As youth faded and I grew older and wiser, I saw the vicar's influence as the first act of grace God gifted to me.

Later, I attended the Kremsmunster Lyceum, where I studied music. In 1811, I had the privilege of studying at Salzburg Seminary. Seminary training persuaded me that those less fortunate in Mariapfarr needed to hear the words of Scripture.

On That Starry Night

In the night hours, long after classes ended, I wrote "Silent Night" ("Stille Nacht"). I purposely wrote it in German rather than in Latin. The year was 1816. If my memory serves me right, I did not leave a trace of written evidence stating the song's inspiration, nor do I remember it now.

What I do remember is my duties as an assistant priest drew me to the pages of Scripture. My heart and mind searched the Word of God, yearning for the truth about this "Holy infant so tender and mild."

Words flowed from my inner being to pen and paper. The song I had written while at Salzburg Seminary remained in my possession. I cherished it, although I had no plans to promote it.

From there, I went to St. Nicholas Church at Oberndorf as assistant priest. I was not favored by the clergy, especially my supervisor, Georg Heinrich Nostler. I was labeled a rebel and often accused of neglecting my duties. He did not care for the fact that my sermons were in German rather than Latin.

With the poverty of my youth embedded in my mind, I could not understand how a sermon preached in Latin would help German people comprehend the truth presented in a foreign language. Tragic, wasted, and shattered lives alienated them from the only hope that could transform them. Without understanding what was preached, change was not possible.

After I graduated from seminary and became an ordained priest, my life and ministry changed. Relationships with parishioners deepened as responsibility increased. I soon learned things rarely change in churches.

Preparing for Christmas in 1818, my first year in the priesthood, I realized the congregation embraced the same carols, Scripture, and practices as in other churches where I had ministered. Troubled, I was determined to surprise the congregation with something new and different.

On the morning of Christmas Eve, the words to the song I wrote at Salzburg Seminary began to fill my mind. I grabbed the music from the old family Bible that had been its hiding place. The paper crumbled as I stuffed it into my pocket. Rushing out the door, I set off to pay a visit to Franz S. Gruber. He was a schoolteacher in the village of Arnsdorf and organist at St. Nicholas Church.

Christmas Eve mass was only hours away. Feeling somewhat reluctant to spring this on my friend with limited time, I asked him to set the song to music so he and I could sing it at the midnight service. I was not sure how he would pull it off. The old organ was broken and had not been played for months, leaving Franz without a musical instrument to test his talent.

As time passed, stories attributing to the demise of the organ flourished. The finest is of a mouse biting through the old church organ's cords, leaving it in disrepair. Another, the organ was old, rusty, and too broken to be played on Christmas Eve. The true story is the Salzach River's continual flooding filled the church and eventually destroyed its exquisite organ.

To my delight, within hours, Franz arranged tempo with notes and presented the music he had written. He knew my love for guitar and composed a melody that complemented the words. Or perhaps, it was knowing the organ was in disrepair that motivated him to write the music for guitar.

The second grace gift took place that cold, starry winter night. Franz and I stood before the small congregation at St. Nicholas Church and, for the first time, sang "Silent Night." Indeed, it was a silent night. Voices hushed as words sprang from our hearts. Silence engulfed the quaint building. The evening was magnificent.

In 1819, after I transferred out of Oberndorf, Karl Mauracher, an organ builder, repaired the old organ. After repairs were completed, Gruber played "Silent Night" to test the instrument. Mauracher was enamored with the song and somehow ended up with a copy of it. I do not know if someone gave it to him, or if he found it in the choir loft. He took it back to his hometown of Zillertal. From there, the song danced its way into the hearts of people in Germany, France, Russia, England, and eventually New York City in 1839.

The third grace gift took place years later. Franz had not been given credit as the composer. His countrymen, known for their love and promotion of music, attributed the composition of the work to Mozart or Beethoven.

Over the years, the original manuscript had been lost. Franz and I had been forgotten. The Royal Prussian Court Chapel in Berlin engaged in research, hoping to find evidence revealing the composer's name.

In 1854, Franz wrote a document to the Royal Prussian Court presenting the work's origin, which endorsed himself as the composer and me as the writer. The court rejected his claim, leaving future attempts useless over the next 150 years.

In 1995, someone found a long-lost arrangement authenticating the author and composer. The manuscript was in my handwriting. In the upper right-hand corner of the parchment, I had written, "Melodie von Fr. Xav. Gruber." My soul was jubilant at the discovery that my good friend, Franz Gruber, had been awarded the title of composer.

Our purpose or intent was not to compose a song that would be loved the world over. However, that is precisely the path the song took across two centuries. The appealing lyrics graced the halls of royalty, brought hope to ghettos, comforted warriors in battle, and was sung in churches of all denominations. This BENEFICIAL BIRTH is a gift of grace from the Holy Infant of Bethlehem, our Savior and King.

DEVOTIONAL

JUST ONE DROP

The great song composer, Gordon Jensen, wrote the lyrics to the song "Written in Red." Jensen's compelling words paint the picture of God's love letter written in crimson. God wrote His love...in blood.

Without the Cross, Jesus' birth would have been reduced to a sweet bedtime story of a baby born in a stable. Imaginations would have the animals lowly whispering during the strange event. Angels would sing lullabies instilling self-esteem and confidence. Stars illuminating the manger would be evidence that the Child is special. But that would not have been a beneficial birth.

Jesus decided to leave Heaven and walk through our communities with us knowing the great agony He would suffer on the Cross. He knew God's requirement, "...without the shedding of blood there is no forgiveness [of sins]" (Hebrews 9:22).

God was talking about the blood of Jesus. Just one drop would have been enough, but the type of death Jesus faced demanded giving of His all. This one act would cause Him to face the greatest disgrace a man could face. When Jesus was crucified, the Father turned away from His Son. In severe anguish, Jesus's final words cried out to His Father, "My God, My God, why have you forsaken me?" (Matthew 27:46). The physical agony was excruciating, but worse was the spiritual separation He endured at His Father's rejection.

Jesus, likewise, experienced the greatest joy that extends beyond what man can experience. The author of Hebrews describes us "...fixing our eyes on Jesus...For the joy set before him he endured the cross, scorning its shame, and sat down at the right hand of the throne of God" (Hebrews 9:22). He did that for you. He did that for me.

The joy that would follow came from Jesus' obedience to His Father—dying on the Cross, rising from the grave three days later, and returning to His original home—Heaven. In doing so, He accomplished his purpose, which opened the path for man's redemption.

The heart of Jesus shared His Father's great love for man. He saw our sinful heart condition and volunteered to die for us. Joy was coming. Jesus experiences that same joy every time a person responds to the plea of the Cross.

God created man for Himself. His desire is for voluntary love to be returned. However, people continually turn inward and do whatever is right in their own thinking. Man excludes

God the Father's great love and precepts that are put in place to protect and provide for him. He has become a lover of self, rejecting God's goodness and compassion. God's Holy character does not allow Him to accept man's reasoning, which leads to dark behavior.

The immeasurable love of God compelled Him to reach out to man in diverse ways and at various times. In the Garden of Eden, God provided the skin of an animal He had killed to cover Adam and Eve's rebellion. Death had to occur and blood had to be shed, which foreshadowed Christ's death for our sin. Before the waters sprang from the earth and fell from the sky, the Lord opened the door of the Ark, but men refused to come in. This, too, foreshadowed the one-way to God—through Jesus Christ—the Door. The Passover lamb became a cultural tradition rather than an acknowledgement of God's great grace and redemption in the promise of the "Lamb of God" who would die for us. In every offer of salvation, man rejected God's plan.

God was extreme. His final invitation to man for salvation was on the Cross of Calvary. He wrote in crimson, "I love you." Then He turned His back as Jesus became our Sin-Bearer.

Jesus is extreme. Jesus agreed to join His Father in providing a way out for sinful man. It is through the voluntary shedding of blood that Jesus became the Savior, the Messiah.

His birth was beneficial. All those who will recognize Him as our Redeemer can call upon His name and receive His great love and forgiveness.

WRITTEN IN RED

It was on a starry night that a young mother laid her new-born baby in a lowly manger. Mary, a virgin, who was highly favored by God, had been told by the angel, Gabriel, that her baby boy would be great and would one day be king. She must have clung to the words as she wrapped Him in swaddling cloth. His birth surely did not make sense to her. Born in a stable and without protective clothes, her baby king did not seem like royalty, but Mary was missing something. She saw the end, but not the in-between.

Jesus was not born to live in a palace. His only purpose was to benefit man. The words of the song "Bring Back the Glory" splendidly declares Jesus is the glory that brings man and God together again. Jesus is the Reconciler, the Savior.

In creation, God's purpose was for man to live. However, before time was, Jesus chose to enter this world not to live, but to die. The birth of Jesus reflects a hint of the cross of Calvary.

Why would a person want to live just long enough to die? Isn't there more to life than death?

Are there not goals to achieve? Cannot fame and wealth be conquered? Does man not have a drive within to reach for the stars? The human heart strives for a higher education, a career of prestige, a spouse and children, wealth, and respect. With all of this before him, why would one Man choose to live so he could die?

In His infinite wisdom and perfect knowledge, this Man knew that every person who ever lived, or would ever live, had overstepped a forbidden line. Jesus knew overstepping the Law of God would carry a price far too high for man to pay, a price that would separate him from God forever.

Was it love that drew Jesus to Earth that star-lit night, so very long ago? The verse, deeply embedded into many a child's mind and heart, is a reminder of God's great love: "For God so loved the world that he gave his one and only Son, that whoever believes in him shall not perish but have eternal life" (John 3:16).

God gave with intention and voluntarily from a heart of love. Before the foundation of the Earth was laid and the first man was created, God saw the debt man would owe. Justice of a Holy God declared Adam, the first person to overstep God's character, guilty of an enormous deficit he could not pay. Everyone who has ever lived inherited that same sin debt.

God purposed to offer an intercessor, His Son. His gift was deliberate. He gave willingly and without reservation. God knew the birth of His Son had to be beneficial to the eternal future of man. He knew man could not build a bridge strong enough, wide enough, or high enough to reach the entrance of Heaven. The gap was too large and too dark. Jesus came down from the splendor of Glory to forge a way for man to enter Heaven and the presence of God. His love bridged the chasm.

The story of a Russian soldier under Emperor Czar Nicholas I's command during the Crimean War (1853-1856) tells of character flaws that identified him as a thief and coward. His punishment was meant to be swift and hard until love bridged the gap.

Because the young man's father was a friend of Czar Nicholas I, he had been given a somewhat responsible post. Each month, it was his responsibility to see that the right amount of money was distributed to soldiers in the barracks. The young man's character was not up to the responsibility. He took to gambling. Eventually, he gambled away a great deal of the government's money and his own.

When the young man noticed that a representative of the Czar was coming to check the accounts, he knew he was in trouble. That evening, he took out the ledger and totaled the funds. He went to the safe and retrieved his pitifully small amount of money. As he sat and compared the two, he was overwhelmed at the astronomical debt versus his insignificant change. He knew he would be disgraced.

When all seemed hopeless, the young man determined to take his life because of the fear of being found out. He yanked out his revolver, placed it on the table before him, and drafted a dissertation of his misdeeds. At the bottom of the ledger, he wrote, "A great debt: who can pay?" He decided to die at the stroke of midnight.

As the evening bore down on him, the young soldier grew drowsy and eventually fell asleep. That night Czar Nicholas I, as was sometimes his custom, made rounds stopping at the barracks. Seeing the glow of the light through the window, he stopped and looked in. He saw the young man asleep and recognized him immediately. Looking over the soldier's shoulder, he saw the journal and considered what had transpired.

He was about to awaken the soldier and put him under arrest when his eyes fastened on the young man's message. "A great debt: who can pay?" With a surge of kindness and love, he reached over, wrote one word at the bottom of the ledger, and slipped out.

The young man awoke abruptly in the middle of the night, glanced at the clock, and realized it was after midnight. As he reached for his revolver, his eye fell upon the ledger. There was his script, "A great debt: who can pay?" Underneath was the word the Czar had written, "Nicholas."

The soldier was dumbfounded. He said to himself, "The Czar has seen the book. He knows all. Still, he is willing to forgive me."

He thought perhaps one of the other soldiers took him for a fool and played a prank on him. He went to the safe where the document that bore the signature of the Czar was on file. He said to himself, "The Czar has seen the book. He knows all. Still, he is willing to forgive me."

He rested on the word of the Czar. The next morning a courier came from the palace with precisely the amount of money needed to meet the deficit. Only the Czar could pay, and he did!

Only the Lord Jesus Christ was able to pay our debt to God. We look at the absolutes of God's righteousness spelled out in His Law. We compare it with our miserable performance and respond, "A great debt to God: who can pay?" But then, the Lord Jesus Christ steps forward and autographs our ledger: "Jesus Christ." Only Jesus can pay, and He did! He still offers that same price today. He shed his blood at Calvary for those who call on His name for the forgiveness of sin.

The birth of Jesus commanded a benefit to man. The damage was too extreme for man to pay. Christ's death and shed blood paid the deficit in full, for you and me. There will be no more debt. His signature is WRITTEN IN RED.

On That Starry Night

A DECORATED BOX

By Melody Chapman
December 1991

The gift of giving is a gift, indeed. To give out of abundance is such a small sacrifice. To give expecting something in return is a gift for self and lacks the element of a full release. A selfless, sacrificial offering, ever so small, is undeniably a gift given from the heart.

This type of giving is rare, but I believe I witnessed it at an early age. Christmas morning, when I was a child, overflowed with wonder and enchantment. It was full of good things to eat and a few new but special possessions.

As an adult, there are occasional quiet times when my mind goes back, and I smell the distinct flavor or combination of oranges and homemade candies, or see the glowing tree lights, or feel the brisk cold of a starlit winter's eve.

It is then that I am reminded of the value of certain ideas I learned as a child. One of those memories helps me to understand that the importance of a gift is relative. From my experiences as a child, I now see that something—anything, even so small—can look immense next to nothing.

My point is, even though nine children shared a tiny four-bedroom home built by my dad and grandfather and we had few possessions, my parents made Christmas magically glitter and gleam through the tool of relativity.

But how did Maggie know? Did she see our car delivery in the dark of night? Did one of us slip and tell a kid? So, Mom asked, and Maggie said there were names on the wrapping paper. The words "To: Melody - From: Linda" had been left on one of the pieces of reused wrapping paper.

This was no small family. The six children were not the most well-kept, well-behaved, or highly respected children. I cannot say that my family was either, but in comparison we looked hopeful.

The kids lacked common etiquette that most people on the poor side of town practiced. Good manners were breached, such as entering your friend's house quietly and respectfully, keeping a Saturday morning visit to just that—not staying until suppertime, and

> A selfless, sacrificial offering, ever so small, is undeniably a gift given from the heart.
>
>

snorting up one's nose rather than using a tissue. I guess you could say they "lived on the other side of the tracks," but then again, so did we.

If I recall correctly, none of us were excited about the project, but maybe it was not the project as much as it was the family. We kids tolerated them despite certain annoyances, and others in town did the same. In contrast, my mother had a way of caring for those in as much need as she. I think that is why so many people called her "friend" and loved her.

We began decorating a box to fill with goodies. Decorating, as in taping used wrapping paper to an old tattered brown box with the lid still attached. Wrapping paper had been saved and used, year after year. My three older sisters carefully peeled the discolored tape off the worn paper and precisely trimmed up the tattered edges. They each had a few years of experience, so they did the job very well. They took turns stretching the well-faded wrapping paper onto the ironing board and pressed the wrinkles out. They did this carefully and slowly because it could scorch or tear easily.

We all carefully checked over the sheets of paper to make sure none of our names were on them. Name tags were a waste of money, which meant someone scribbled the giver and receiver's names on the wrapping paper. We each had a job to do, and we were expected to do it well as we carefully wrapped boots, toy guns, jacks, bubble bath, and other treasures. We viewed and touched them with a mixture of curiosity and a little bit of envy.

One of my older brothers loaded a cap gun to pop, but Mom intercepted, "You will not shoot that! It is a gift to give away."

We worked together until each of the six children and their mother and father had a gift carefully wrapped and arranged in the colorfully dressed box. We filled the rest of it with nuts, candy, and fruit until it was overflowing.

By this point in the evening, we children had become excited. Any reluctance we once had melted away like snow on a warm day. We, along with our mother, piled into a small car, and my oldest sister drove slowly down the dark, deserted country road. It seemed like a longer drive on that cold evening, and we chattered all the way. Suspense filled us. Who would deliver the box to the door? What if the dog barked? How could we turn the car lights off and get back to it quickly in the dark without being caught red-handed?

As we slowly approached, my sister crowded the half-acre yard, driving as close to the house as she dared. She turned off the car headlights but left the engine running for a fast get-away.

One of my little sisters and I were chosen to help mom carry the box closer to the house. The dogs began to bark, but we snuck through the night up to the front door like Indians in the woods, trying not to snap a twig.

We quietly dropped the box on the front porch and ran through the dark, each of us finding our spot back in the car. We caught a glimpse of the front door slowly opening as my big sister drove the car away onto the moonlit road. With car lights still off and whispering excitement for a job well done, we headed down the back roads to our noisy little home in our quiet small town.

We'd accomplished our great mission, and the adventure was memorable. The quiet chatter in the car was different as each of us promised and double promised that we would not say a word about our spirited night when we saw the family again. We would not even crack a smile.

For me, it was all fun and excitement, and keeping it a secret was a challenge. Christmas Day at our house came and went. I do not especially remember my gift that year, but I do not remember feeling cheated out of anything either. I do recall sharing in the joy of the quiet, sacrificial giving my mom embraced.

A strange twist took place after a few days passed, and the family visited our home. My brothers and sisters and I tried to act calm and collected. Maggie, the family's mother, said they got a surprise Christmas box delivered on their step one evening, and she knew it was from our mom. Mother was surprised and tried to hide a smile as she briefly acted innocent. She felt exposed and let down because she wanted the gifts to be anonymous. She did not want to humiliate or embarrass her friend by making her think she appeared needy.

But how did Maggie know? Did she see our car delivery in the dark of night? Did one of us slip and tell a kid? So, Mom asked, and Maggie said there were names on the wrapping paper. The words "to Stephanie from Mark" had been left on one of the pieces of reused wrapping paper.

In the eyes of a child, here was the amazing thing to me. My mom gave that year to a family the people in our small town looked down upon and despised. They were a family that needed a friend. They considered my mom to be their friend. Even as a child, I could see that my mother wanted nothing in return that Christmas. Her only desire was to see someone in need blessed through her giving. Hers was a sacrificial gift of selflessness. What Mom may not have been thinking about is the influence it had on her children. As each of us was a part of giving that year, the experience helped influence who we were to become and how we live and give.

We are grown now. When my four children were teens, my young family gave comparably to a needy family. We also gave anonymously as we secretly delivered a carefully assembled box of goods one chilly, starlit evening. I was truly blessed this time as I watched my children sneak the box and leave it on a chosen doorstep. As I remembered my adventure from years ago, I quietly hoped this new act of kindness would affect my children in a unique and lasting way.

As I reflected and questioned my motives that evening, the thought came to me that, like myself, my mother was sharing a taste of the gift we were all given on that beautiful first Christmas Day—an exciting gift known as Immanuel, God with us. God surprised the world, and sacrificially sent us the baby Jesus. He was given to us so we, even in our poverty and weakness, through the promise of the Master Giver, are equipped to provide to those in need.

*Now would be an excellent time for you to write about a memory of love.
Who impacted your life with just one act of kindness?*

DEVOTIONAL THREE: A BENEFICIAL BIRTH

MY STORY

DATE: _____
AUTHOR: _____
TITLE: _____

DEVOTIONAL FOUR

A LOWLY BIRTH

DURING THE FOURTH devotional, a different attribute emerges—humility. Unlike the first three attributes, this one is a human as well as a divine characteristic. We will get a glimpse of the humbleness of Jesus as the Lamb of God. Lighting the pink Humility candle symbolizes Jesus doing the will of His Father.

A humble pastor discovered the "awe" of Bethlehem from a hillside overlooking the place where Jesus lay on that first Christmas night. In the Christmas carol, "O, Little Town of Bethlehem," the author tells of the quietness that settled over the town when Jesus was born.

"The Christmas Window" takes us to another place and another time. The story tells of a struggling mother with whom many women identify. She did not allow her own misfortunes to prevent her from reaching out to others in love.

O, Little Town of Bethlehem
Phillips Brooks
12/12/1835-01/23/1893
Year: 1868
Composer: Lewis Henry Redner
Year: 1868

As Pastor Phillips Brooks of Holy Trinity Church in Philadelphia, I was given the amazing privilege and opportunity of visiting the Holy Land during Advent. My heart and mind were captivated by the country's beauty and the magnificent history of the people.

Memories of the trip "still sang in my soul" as I sat at my office desk. Recollections of my experience are alive and vivid.

In December 1865, I was riding on horseback from Jerusalem to Bethlehem on Christmas Eve. As the evening grew dark and cold, I stopped at the Field of the Shepherds and watched as the stars began to envelop the little village of Bethlehem. The solitude and majesty of the night sky held me captive.

As the evening slipped away, I began to wonder if I should have left hours ago, for I planned to be in Bethlehem to preach at the Church of the Nativity for the Christmas Eve service. I did not know the number of hours that passed. I hurriedly and reluctantly gathered my bag, mounted my horse, and continued my journey to Bethlehem.

As I approached the secluded town, I distinctly remember the harmony of melodious songs resounding through the darkness, drowning out the cries of hungry cows, sheep, and horses that anxiously waited for dinner. In silence, I slipped off my horse and stepped through the crafted cedar door of the ancient church. I quietly stood by the church's entrance observing and listening as sweet angelic voices sang the story of the glorious night of our dear Savior's birth.

When I returned to Philadelphia, the memories slept in my heart for three years. In the winter of 1868, shortly before Christmas, I wrote the words to "O Little Town of Bethlehem" for the children's annual play.

Lewis Redner, our church organist, was given the task of writing the music. He had little time because the pageant was just days away.

Redner tried for a week to put music to the words but failed. I was becoming nervous and increasingly concerned. Early, on the morning of Christmas Eve, Redner rushed into my office, declaring, "Miraculously, last night, I suddenly awoke from my sleep and quickly wrote the music that was dancing in my head."

He described the experience as "a gift from heaven."

For the first time that evening, the captivating lyrics softly awakened the hearts of the people to the mystery of Christ's birth. As the carol made its way into churches, homes, and theaters over the next two centuries, the warmth and peace still linger. It echoes the truth of Christ's LOWLY BIRTH that took place on that starlit night in the little town of Bethlehem.

DEVOTIONAL

"BEHOLD, THE LAMB OF GOD!"

The morning sun broke through the white floating clouds as John the Baptist slumped onto the grass to await the gathering crowd. His camel hair tunic was soaked in the damp morning dew. John thought of God's mission, a message of hope to the Jewish people. He preached a baptism of repentance for the forgiveness of sin and was instructed to announce the coming of the Lamb of God. He pondered the many people who had responded to his message by confessing their sins and being baptized.

He then thought of Jewish religious and political leaders. They did not accept his message, because it challenged their teachings about God and the Law. They became angry and fearful of losing influence and power.

The crowd was gathering.

Stepping into the Jordan River, John said, "17 For the law was given through Moses; grace and truth came through Jesus Christ. 18 No one has ever seen God, but the one and only Son, who is himself God and is in closest relationship with the Father, has made him known" (John 1:17-18).

John did not fear the Jewish people who disagreed with him. They did as he expected and went to the priest and Levites to report his claim that Jesus was God.

John's voice raised as the Jewish leaders approached. "Repent, for the Kingdom of God is coming soon. Isaiah, the prophet, told you of Him. He is more powerful than I am. I am not worthy enough to stoop down and untie His sandals. I can baptize you with water, but He will baptize you with the Holy Spirit."

The religious leaders pushed their way to the river's edge, pressing John for answers to his claim, "I am not the Messiah."

They shouted, "Then, who are you?" "Are you Elijah?" "Are you the prophet?" "Who are you?" "Give us an answer! We need to know."

He boldly confessed, "No. I am not the Messiah" (John 1:15-35).

The following day John had the opportunity to introduce Jesus to the crowd. "Look, the Lamb of God, who takes away the sin of the world!" (John 1:29).

John had recently baptized Jesus. His baptism marked the beginning of His public life. As He came up out of the water, the Spirit of God came as a dove and rested on Jesus, identifying Him as the Son of God.

Heaven opened, and God spoke, "This is my Son, whom I love; with him I am well pleased" (Matthew 3:17).

When John shouted, "Behold!" he acknowledged the admiration and wonderment of the Man. John's desire was for people to embrace three truths about Christ: Jesus is the precious Lamb, the provided Lamb, and the perfect Lamb of God.

John cried out, "This is the One I spoke about when I said, 'He who comes after me has surpassed me because he was before Me'" (John 1:15).

He referred to eternity past, a time before time was. Jesus was the precious Lamb of God in eternity past. God and Jesus lived together, worked together, planned together, and laughed together for ever, and ever, and ever.

Their relationship was intimate to the degree that Jesus said, "[19]...the Son can do nothing by himself; he can do only what he sees his Father doing, because whatever the Father does the Son also does. [20] For the Father loves the Son and shows him all he does" (John 5:19-20). They existed in complete accord for trillions of centuries if centuries could be counted in eternity.

> As He came out of the water, the Spirit of God came as a dove and rested on Him, identifying Him as the Son of God.

Occasionally, a couple celebrates seventy years of marriage. Even though their relationship has stood the test of time, at some point someone is hurt, lied to, taken advantage of, or disappointed. More common are commitments that fail after five to ten years. In both cases, united hearts are broken and in need of healing. To think a couple could live together for centuries without brokenness is unthinkable.

God and Jesus never had a broken relationship. The Father was never neglectful, abusive, or unkind. The Son was obedient, respectful, and listened to His Father. Their relationship was sealed in a depth of love we cannot know.

When Jesus fulfilled His ministry on Earth, God expressed His delight, pleasure, love, and satisfaction with His Son one last time. On the Mount of Transfiguration, God repeated, "This is my Son, whom I love; with him I am well pleased" (Matthew 17:5).

Jesus, beloved and precious, was transported from this world by His loving Father to a different dimension. He took His place at the right side of His Father in Heaven. There He sits with thousands upon thousands, and ten thousand times tens of thousands of angels singing, "Worthy is the Lamb, who was slain, to receive power and wealth and wisdom and strength and honor and glory and praise!" (Revelation 5:12).

In Heaven, the Father looks into the eyes of His precious Son and delights in the One whom He loves. Jesus was not only the precious Lamb, He was also the provided Lamb.

God promised Abraham and his wife, Sarah, a son. After twenty-five years of waiting, when they were too old to have children, God gave them a son.

When Isaac was fifteen, God tested Abraham's faith. More importantly, God planned for Abraham and Isaac's relationship to have a significant purpose that would influence people throughout the centuries. He wanted them to get a glimpse of His love for Jesus and the great sacrifice He gave when Jesus dies on the Cross.

God asked Abraham to bear a dreadful burden—to sacrifice his and Sarah's only son. Abraham took Isaac, wood, fire, and a knife and built an altar. Isaac asked his father, "But where is the lamb...?"

Abraham replied, "The Lord will provide a lamb."

At that very moment, Abraham heard a rustling behind him. He turned, lifted his eyes, and looked. A ram was entangled in a thicket by his horns. Abraham took the animal and offered it as a burnt offering instead of his son. The God of the Universe provided the lamb.

Abraham's ram framed a picture of Jesus, the only Son of God, as the Sacrificial Lamb given by God. The apostle Peter explained it carefully. "[18] For you know that it was not with perishable things such as silver or gold that you were redeemed... [19] but with the precious blood of Christ, a lamb without blemish or defect. [20] He was chosen before the creation of the world, but was revealed in these last times for your sake" (I Peter 1:18-20).

God provided His precious Son as the perfect Lamb of God who "takes away the sins of the world."

The book of Exodus tracks the Jewish people to Egypt where they lived in captivity as slaves for 430 years. God had plans for them. He wanted them freed from Egypt, but Pharoah had other plans. He wanted the Israelites to continue building his kingdom. He needed slaves.

God appointed Moses to lead the Israelites into a life of freedom. But, Pharoah refused to let the people go free. In His grace, God gave Pharaoh ten opportunities to change his mind with the last one being a plague on each family's firstborn. Moses' plea to Pharaoh was to free God's people. If he refused, God would send the Death Angel to slay the firstborn son in every Egyptian house. How could a loving God commit such atrocity?

Throughout the ages, God provided a way out—a way of escape from His justice. He did the same for Pharaoh and the Egyptian people. In chapters 11 and 12 of Exodus, God tells how He provided the Passover Lamb as a means of escape from His pending judgment.

God provided the Passover Lamb as a sacrifice for Pharaoh's past refusal of releasing the Israelite people. His provision was a means of convincing Pharaoh that he would face judgment if he refused to do things God's way. Pharaoh needed only to believe that what God had said was true, and to act on it. However, his decisions were based on what he felt served himself best at the time.

God made it clear. He told Moses to inform Pharaoh of His intent. "[4]About midnight I will go throughout Egypt. [5] Every firstborn son in Egypt will die,..." (Exodus 11:4-5) [*unless* you let My people go."] But Pharaoh refused to believe God.

God gave instructions to Moses in choosing a Passover Lamb. The lamb had to be perfect, free of defects. After killing the lamb, blood was to be put on the sides and tops of the doorframe of the Israelites' homes.

God spoke, "On that same night I will pass through Egypt and strike down every firstborn..., and I will bring judgment on all the gods of Egypt. I am the LORD. The blood will be a sign for you on the houses where you are, and when I see the blood, I will pass over you" (Exodus 12:12-13).

It is the Lord's Passover. The Israelites would not see death that night because they were protected under the blood of the Lamb.

When Jesus hung on the Cross, the Jewish nation clearly understood the spiritual significance of the lamb. Under God's direction, the ceremonial lamb was to be a one-year-old male without scratches, bruises, broken bones, or tainted wool. One black dot on one strain of wool disqualified the lamb. Its eyesight could not be blurred, nor its hearing faint. God demanded perfection of the sacrificial lamb. A perfect sacrifice was the only justification a Holy God could accept for the sinful nature of man.

Jesus is the perfect Lamb of God without blemish or defect (I Peter 1:19). Those who have put their faith in Jesus are under the blood of Christ (Ephesians 1:7). Jesus is the perfect Passover Lamb "who takes away the sins of the world." The apostle Paul wrote, "For Christ, our Passover lamb, has been sacrificed" (I Corinthians 5:7).

The sacrifice of the Lamb of God should move our hearts toward Him, not away from Him, in praise and worship. We should be amazed at His awesome glory.

LAMB OF HOPE

The Earthly heritage of our Lord was not one to be envied. He came from a genealogy of harlots, adulteresses, and unfaithful men: Tamar, Rahab, Bathsheba, Abraham, Jacob, and King David. With a heart of humbleness, Mary—the mother of Jesus—referred to herself as nothing more than a handmaid. Royalty was not her pedigree. Joseph—the man who raised Jesus—was a carpenter, humble and ordinary.

The King of Glory stepped down from His Father's throne to a world He could not call His own. He did not have a royal home birth in a palace with highly qualified doctors and nurses. In the quiet of the night, a dark, damp stable was His birthplace. Unlike a royal birth, there was no official news release made by the town crier for all to hear. The announcement of Jesus' birth was by heavenly angels to lowly, uneducated, smelly shepherds who were awed and rejoiced at the birth of this little one. There was no silk finery provided for this newborn baby. His sleeper was a swaddling cloth. There were no celebrations, no baby shower, no flowers, balloons, or banners. His carpenter "dad" and humble mom treasured the moments of His lowly birth without family or friends.

Jesus entered the world in humility as the Lamb of God. The apostle Paul wrote in Philippians

2:6-7: "Who [Jesus], being in the very nature God, did not consider equality with God something to be used to his own advantage; rather, he made himself nothing by taking the very nature of a servant, being made in human likeness."

Becoming a man did not rob Jesus of His deity. Humility did not rob Him of His strength and power.

As the humble birth of the Babe of Bethlehem brought hope to the Jewish people and ultimately to the world, so does the Lamb of God bring hope into our individual lives. The birth of Jesus was the fulfillment of the prophesied Messiah, The Anointed One. The Jewish nation yearned for a ruler, a king, who could destroy their captors, set them free, and restore the nation of Israel. The Messiah was their hope, but they rejected Him. Through His sacrificial death, The Lamb of God brings hope into the hearts of people who find themselves ruled by fear of an eternity they do not understand.

As John the Baptist shouted, "[Behold,] the Lamb of God [who takes away the sin of the world!]" (John 1:36), so does the Lamb of God call us. Jesus said, "I am the way and the truth and the life. No one comes to the Father except through me" (John 14:6). Jesus brought hope of eternal life to all people. Each person has a decision to make, receive the Lamb of God as Lord and Savior, or reject His great gift of salvation

On That Starry Night

DEVOTIONAL FOUR: A LOWLY BIRTH

THE CHRISTMAS WINDOW

Come! Come with me!

Step back in time. Look through the window of Christmas as we walk down Main Street in a small, mid-west country town on Christmas Eve.

Do you see frost, sparkling like diamonds, settling on storefront windows as the sun sets behind the buildings? Unlike other nights, Christmas lights, casting a soft glow through windows, remain lit as late Christmas shoppers leave the boutiques, dime stores, and shops frustrated; they could not find the perfect gift at the right price.

Doors are closed and locked as business owners step into the cold, starry night, nodding and waving as they wish each other a "Merry Christmas." Car engines sputter before the doors slam shut, and seat belts are fasten. The race home, despite icy roads, seems longer tonight because family and friends have already gathered to enjoy the holidays.

As we stroll through the quaint town, we enjoy the beauty of homes illuminated with white, green, red, and multicolored lights, which provide a picture frame for the decorated Christmas trees stationed perfectly in the windows.

Take a quick peek through the front window of the houses. You might catch a glimpse of a family gathered by the fireplace waiting for Grandfather to tell stories of his childhood Christmases. The aroma of gingerbread cookies fills the air while Grandmother serves hot cider to small children snuggled in flannel PJs with prints of Santa Claus and his reindeer, decorated Christmas trees, and silver stars on blue fabric. The young ones are excitedly shaking decorated boxes in hopes of discovering hidden treasure imprisoned by wrapping paper, ribbon, and bows.

Now, follow me on this Christmas Eve adventure to 312 Central Street, where a different story unfolds. The house you see has no lights on the window framing the Christmas tree. Spindly branches, unevenly distributed, droop, touching the old wood floor while a rusty gallon green bean can is an unsteady tree-stand, causing the evergreen to tilt slightly to the right. The fishing line secured from the tree to the curtain rod is the anchor that keeps it from toppling to the floor.

In the living room, by the oil stove, a young mother says to her older children, "Quickly put on your coat, hat, boots, and gloves," as she bundles the younger children in their winter clothes.

After the older children wrap themselves for the winter's eve walk, the mother hands three small cardboard boxes containing twelve brown paper bags overstuffed with homemade cookies, sheets of simple; yet elegant stationery with matching envelopes, a pencil, and a red and white candy cane, to the three older girls. The young mother tucks her beautiful black hair under her scarf and slips into her tattered coat as she rushes her children out the door into the frigid night air.

Follow the family up Central Street, make a left turn, walk three short blocks, make a right turn, and stop in front of a faded, white, vintage house with stairs leading to the front door. With conflicting excitement and apprehension, the younger kids race up the steps to see whose finger will hit the doorbell first. A wrinkled-faced woman with shaking hands and weak, bowed knees cracks open the door and peeks out. Without uttering a sound, she slams the door leaving the wide-eyed children speechless and alarmed. After what seemed like forever, but was seconds later, a younger woman opens the door, smiles, and warmly welcomes her visitors.

The children's eyes scan the older people sitting in the living room. The youngsters surmise that most appear to be kind and harmless as others carry a hint of discomfort. Regardless, the children know their tasks. Gingerly taking a brown paper bag from the box, they offer each senior a gift. With quivering hands, the elderly strain to reach their prize. Smiles, laughter, and small conversation follow.

After every man and woman in the sitting room have slowly and curiously investigated the delicacies, the children quietly and slowly wander down the corridor and stop at every bedroom. They offer bags to the frail ones lying in beds or tied securely in chairs to keep them from falling. Before long, the boxes are empty, and the bags are gone. One thing remains; the smiles and tears of joy that sprinkle the faces of the aged.

Our journey is complete. As the family walks into the star-lit night, the young mother, without realizing it, had given her children a far greater gift than what she gave to the elderly. Hers reached into the lives and souls of her children as they experienced gift-giving through her humble and sacrificial heart—one that touched the lonely, needy, and sick lives of desperate people.

On this Christmas eve, the rickety house no longer stands, and there are no windows to look through. All is gone except for the heart-changing memories stamped in the lives of those who lived there. But upon reflection, one realizes the innocence of childhood prevents kids from asking certain questions—questions that were never thought or meant to be asked but later surface as adults and haunt us. If only it were possible, perhaps the relevant question today would be, "Mother, how did you get the money to purchase those gifts?"

DEVOTIONAL FOUR: A LOWLY BIRTH

Do you have a story when you sacrificially gave to someone who was in need and looked down upon by your community?

Drafting your story would preserve that memory for years to come.

DEVOTIONAL FIVE
A ROYAL BIRTH

ROYALTY, CHARACTERIZED BY the purple candle, is the theme of the fifth and final week of Advent. The focus of this devotional is Jesus as King. The title "King" refers to a sovereign authority by right of birth—someone who has great power and glory. Christ will come as King of Kings and Lord of Lords.

The Christmas carol "Joy to The World" is a splendid way to end the Advent Season. The anticipation of seeing Jesus should cause our hearts to soar. At an early age, the author of the carol prepared his heart for the newborn King. Christ's birth dims slightly as we ponder the Second Coming of our LORD to Earth and prepare to receive our glorious King.

A hush should settle over our homes on Christmas Eve as the magnificent story of the birth of Jesus is read from Scripture. The book of Matthew is Joseph's story. Luke steps into Mary's heart and tells the events she pondered the night her baby was born.

DEVOTIONAL FIVE: A ROYAL BIRTH

Joy to the World
Isaac Watts
07/17/1674-11/25/1748
Year: 1719
Composer:
Dr. Lowell Mason
Year: 1839

I grew up carrying the name of my father, Isaac Watts, which provided me with nothing more than a shadowy beginning. Being raised in Southampton, Hampshire, England, was not easy because my father was a man known for nonconformist beliefs. He was a religious man whose extreme worldview caused him to reject the Church of England and resulted in his imprisonment more than once. When he was not in jail, he spent time making me miserable by challenging me to higher excellence.

My father's eccentric theology disqualified me from being accepted into schools in which I could have excelled. Oxford and Cambridge college education was not for people of my social status.

Instead, my early education took place at home, where I mastered theology and languages. Each morning, my father purposely instructed studies in biblical doctrine and assured me that I had a keen understanding of the principles and precepts taught.

My sweet mother realized that I had the acute gift of hearing sounds, remembering them, and applying meaning to words. At the age of five, she challenged me to accelerate my Latin classes. When I turned nine, my mom thought me mature and bright enough to learn Greek. French was acquired at eleven, followed by Hebrew, which I conquered during my thirteenth year.

As a young boy, I realized I had a propensity for rhyme. One Sunday morning, an older man at church asked me why I did not close my eyes during prayers. I responded, "A little mouse for want of stairs ran up a rope to say its prayers." My father disapproved of my answer and decided discipline was in line. In desperation and trying to avoid a harsh hand on my backside, I shouted, "O father, father, pity take, and I will no more verses make." To my sorrow, that did not change my father's decision.

I enjoyed studying and rhyming, but that love did not spill over into the music I had to endure each Sunday morning at church. I often complained to my father about the music; he challenged me to write something better.

As early as I remember, my soul panted for the truths of Scripture. At sixteen, I began studying theology at Dissenting Academy at Stoke Newington and eventually obtained a degree that led me into ministry. Days were often long, demanding, and stressful; however, when evening shadows fell and silence settled over the house, I found a hiding place at the home of Thomas Abney and the Lady Mary.

In Lady Mary's garden, elm trees chaperoned me to the Hackney Brook where I found solitude, and allowed my heart to flood blank pages with hymns inspired by the Psalms.

The result was a revolution in church music as the 750 hymns I wrote made their way into church worship services. Psalm 98 spurred me to pen the verses to "Joy to the World." The intent was not for it to be a Christmas carol, but rather, a poetic expression of an old Jewish psalm of praise that spoke of the Second Coming of Christ. The first publication appeared in my book of poems, *The Psalms of David Imitated*, published in 1719. A century later, Dr. Lowell Mason put the words to music.

The Psalm and song dictate a tone of rejoicing for the coming of the King. An invitation is offered for humankind to prepare his heart for the magnificent event. Written within the lyrics is a reminder that God's love and faithfulness to His people are eternal. An acknowledgment of salvation provided by God through His Son, Jesus, is revealed and provides a glimpse of the unfolding drama of redemption.

It began in the garden and reached beyond the Babe of Bethlehem to an eternal Kingdom that will be declared when the entire world bows the knee to celebrate His return to Earth. His coming would not be possible without HIS ROYAL BIRTH.

DEVOTIONAL

A LION'S CUB

Hundreds of thousands of pharaohs, monarchs, chieftains, czars, presidents, and kings have walked the halls of majestic buildings. Each lived their story of power, dominance, and wealth. Before their reign, they were warriors, princes, senators, and heads of state. They were masterminds behind coups and candidates of integrity who rose from poverty and unforeseen circumstance. Narcissistic rulers pursued thrones of peaceful kings. Sovereigns with extraordinary wisdom, decency, and high standards sought kingdoms of peace.

Each left a legacy be it grand or grueling. The way they lived their lives and ruled their subjects were recorded in the scrolls of history. Ages after death snatched their final breath, annals speak of who they were.

In Genesis 49:9-10, Jacob blessed his son, Judah, by telling him God had chosen him to be the ancestor of Israel's line of the kings: "⁹You are a lion's cub, Judah;... ¹⁰ The scepter will not depart from Judah, nor the ruler's staff from between his feet, until he to whom it belongs shall come..." God established Judah [Israel] as the first in the royal line of the nation of Israel. Judah is the lion's cub, the foreshadow of Jesus, the Lion of Judah.

The shepherd boy, David, was God's first anointed man for the position of king. King David came from the line of Judah and was promised his kingdom would never end.

> ¹² When your days are over and you rest with your ancestors, I will raise up your offspring to succeed you, your own flesh and blood, and I will establish his kingdom. ¹³ He is the one who will build a house for my Name, and I will establish the throne of his kingdom forever (2 Samuel 7:12-13).

In the book of Luke, the author brings attention to Joseph's heritage from David's lineage. Centuries passed, and the kingly line was not broken. From David—the descendent of Judah, the lion's cub—to Jesus—the Lion of the Tribe of Judah—God has kept His promise.

Israel crowned king after king making each one ruler of the people. Jesus was born King. He did not have to be crowned King. Matthew chapter two records the Magi asking King Herod where they could find the one born "King of the Jews." Jesus is the King from the lion's cub.

At the end of His stay on Earth, Jesus was asked by Pontius Pilate the true nature of His Kingdom. Jesus made it clear that His kingdom is not on Earth but in Heaven.

> "You are a king, then?" Pilate said.
> Jesus answered, "You say that I am a king. In fact, the reason I was born and came into the world is to testify to the truth…" (John 18:37).

Jesus embraced His kingly coronation as a crown of thorns was placed on His head. He knew His followers would lose sight of the heavenly kingdom about which He taught. Not only did they dismiss the knowledge and reality of the kingdom, but they became fearful and ashamed to be associated with their King. His disciples were short-sighted and could not see beyond the horror of the night. They refused to stand with the One who loved them. They defected and abandoned Him to the loneliness of the Cross.

Jesus went to the cross, not as King but as the Lamb of God, meek and willing to die in obedience to His Father.

Jesus went to the Cross, not as King but as the Lamb of God, meek and willing to die in obedience to His Father. His motivation was love. It was at Calvary that Jesus became the Great Sin-Bearer.

Jesus did not demand or yearn for power, wealth, or control, as did kings before Him. He intentionally determined to endure the Cross knowing the journey to death would lead to a deeper state of darkness for Him. His holy and just Father could not look at His Son because of our sin He carried to Calvary. The iniquities of all people were on Him. His Father turned and deserted Jesus to bear the agony without Him. His accusers and murderers nailed a sign on the Cross that read, "King of the Jews". His royalty was acknowledged while He hung on the Tree.

Death could not bind Him. Love empowered Him to come forth from the grave as Victorious King. Today He dwells in His Heavenly Kingdom, but He is not silent on Earth. He reigns as the "Wonderful Counselor, Mighty God, Everlasting Father, Prince of Peace" (Isaiah 9:6). The King reaches down when the storms of life have tossed us into depths of misery. He is our Peacemaker, the Anchor for our minds and emotions, and a loving Father who hugs us until our pain dwindles. And He is Almighty God!

We should not view Christ's return to Earth merely as a hope for escaping this present darkness. Instead, His Word should beckon us to embrace each day as a Holy Day and an opportunity to direct others to know Him.

THE LION'S ROAR

From Adam to Joseph the Carpenter, men-and-women-of-old looked with expectancy and hopefulness for the Messiah's birth. Those who put their faith in the person of Jesus look with anticipation to the Second Advent of Christ. The second time He comes to Earth, He will come as the conquering King in power and great glory—the King of Kings and Lord of Lords.

His title as King was not an earthly inherited one carried down through generations. His character is that of a king, majestic and glorious. He did not leave that position in Heaven. He did, however, choose to live as a humble carpenter's son while on Earth. No one is born a king. A prince becomes a king upon his father's death, but Christ was King—Ruler of the Universe, before He walked among men. He does not rule as a dictator but in love. Henry Lockyer states it well in his book *The Messianic Prophecies of the Bible*: "He rules by love, and sways our souls, not by a sword, but by His scars. His suffering brought Him sovereignty. Triumph is His because of the Tree."

Jesus displayed His ultimate power when He died on the Tree—the Cross. The Cross shrieked of the wicked power the Roman Empire possessed to take the life of any person they chose and for any reason. The Cross exposed the secret of the Jewish leaders' spiritual insecurity when tradition was challenged and mindsets opposed. Jesus could have come down from the Cross with one spoken word. Instead, He accepted the power His Father gave him to bear the agony that was before Him. Love, the greatest strength of all, kept Jesus on the Cross.

He does not use His power to push Himself into our lives. Jesus does not manipulate His way into our world with the sword of narcissism, seeking control, and needing to be the center of attention. He does not demand love in return for giving His life. Jesus told His story to the apostles centuries ago. He said with love that He came to seek and to save those who were lost.

God's character remains the same today; it has not changed. Christ comes to us with honor and dignity, gently knocking at our door. As a gentleman pursuing His lover, Jesus holds Himself forth as the fragrant, beautiful, and perfect "Rose of Sharon" for us to take as our own. As we cradle the Rose in our hand, His love compels us to give up our rights to love another and to live in abandonment to Him, the "Lover of Our Soul." He sways us with His love!

"Triumph is His because of the Tree," Lockyer states. Were it not for the Cross and the shedding of blood, Jesus's kingly right would have ended at Calvary. He would have traveled death's valley as have all earth's fallen kings, leaving lost kingdoms and ancient graves. The Sacrificial Lamb was slain on the Cross and laid in a dark, cold tomb. Three days later, after an angel rolled away the tombstone, the conquering Lamb of God stepped over the threshold in His glorified body.

The Lion of the Tribe of Judah was victorious over the grave and destroyed His enemies because it was not possible for death to hold Him (Acts 2:24). Satan heard His roar and trembled at the sound.

One day, Jesus Christ will establish a new kingdom on Earth, one of peace which man has yearned for throughout the centuries, especially the Jews. This kingdom will not crumble at the hand of the mightiest army. There will be total peace under the reign of the Lion of Judah.

Before Christ's declares His reign, He is going to roar the second time, and the sound will not be limited to five miles like it is with the King of the Jungle. Every nation and person will hear and know to look upward. There will be absolutely no doubt as to who He is as He descends to earth. His enemies will surrender and fall to their knees at His name. When He establishes His rule here, there will be no weeping, pain, divorce, drug overdoses or drunken parents. Revelation 5:5 reads, "Do not weep! See, the Lion of the Tribe of Judah, the Root of David, has triumphed."

King Jesus will come in glory and majesty and govern with compassion and justice. He will bring deliverance and destroy the consequences of when Adam and Eve chose to be their own god and do things their way. He will restore creation and bring everlasting peace.

As anticipation swells within us tonight at the celebration of the birth of the Sacrificial Lamb of God, let us, with the same expectancy and excitement, look forward to the coming of the King of Kings and Lord of Lords. The Lion of the Tribe of Judah ROARS!

DEVOTIONAL FIVE: A ROYAL BIRTH

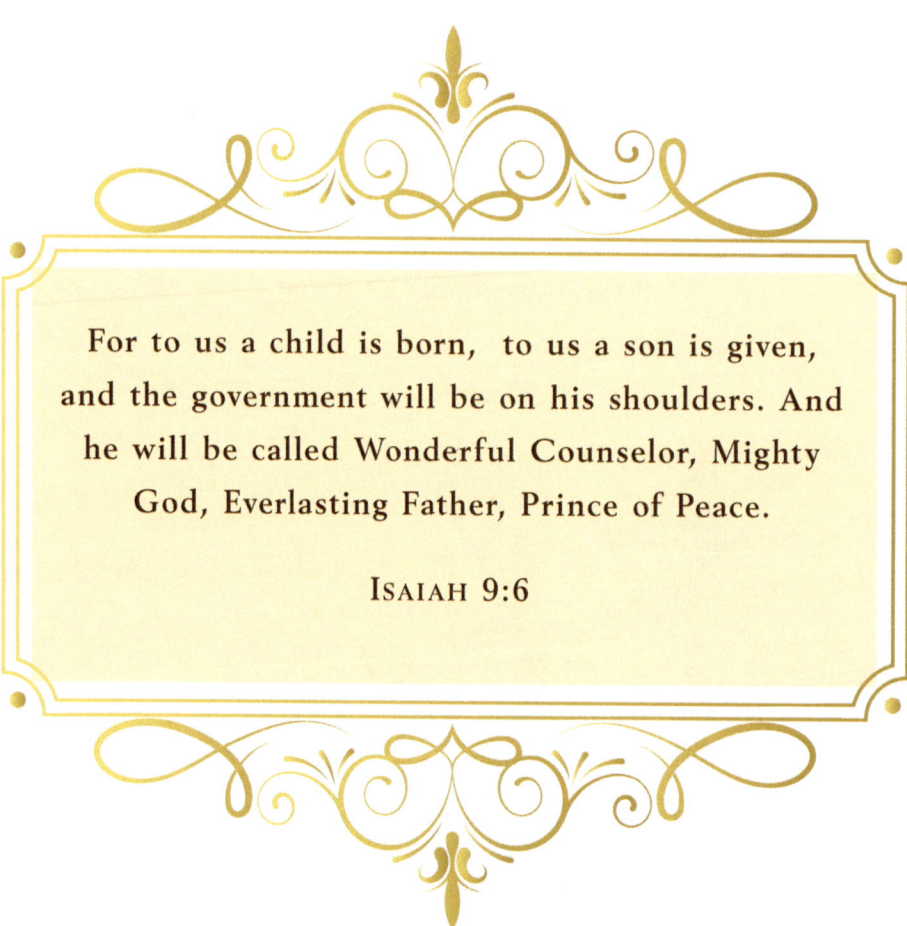

For to us a child is born, to us a son is given, and the government will be on his shoulders. And he will be called Wonderful Counselor, Mighty God, Everlasting Father, Prince of Peace.

Isaiah 9:6

BIRTH OF THE KING

MARY'S STORY—PART 1 (LUKE 1:5-38)

The Birth of John the Baptist Foretold

5 IN THE TIME of Herod king of Judea there was a priest named Zechariah, who belonged to the priestly division of Abijah; his wife Elizabeth was also a descendant of Aaron. **6** Both of them were righteous in the sight of God, observing all the Lord's commands and decrees blamelessly. **7** But they were childless because Elizabeth was not able to conceive, and they were both very old.

8 Once when Zechariah's division was on duty and he was serving as priest before God, **9** he was chosen by lot, according to the custom of the priesthood, to go into the temple of the Lord and burn incense. **10** And when the time for the burning of incense came, all the assembled worshipers were praying outside.

11 Then an angel of the Lord appeared to him, standing at the right side of the altar of incense. **12** When Zechariah saw him, he was startled and was gripped with fear. **13** But the angel said to him: "Do not be afraid, Zechariah; your prayer has been heard. Your wife Elizabeth will bear you a son, and you are to call him John. ¹⁴ He will be a joy and delight to you, and many will rejoice because of his birth, ¹⁵ for he will be great in the sight of the Lord. He is never to take wine or other fermented drink, and he will be filled with the Holy Spirit even before he is born. ¹⁶ He will bring back many of the people of Israel to the Lord their God. ¹⁷ And he will go on before the Lord, in the spirit and power of Elijah, to turn the hearts of the parents to their children and the disobedient to the wisdom of the righteous—to make ready a people prepared for the Lord."

¹⁸ Zechariah asked the angel, "How can I be sure of this? I am an old man, and my wife is well along in years."

¹⁹ The angel said to him, "I am Gabriel. I stand in the presence of God, and I have been sent to speak to you and to tell you this good news. ²⁰ And now you will be silent and not able to speak until the day this happens, because you did not believe my words, which will come true at their appointed time."

²¹ Meanwhile, the people were waiting for Zechariah and wondering why he stayed so long in the temple. ²² When he came out, he could not speak to them. They realized he had seen a vision in the temple, for he kept making signs to them but remained unable to speak.

²³ When his time of service was completed, he returned home. ²⁴ After this his wife Elizabeth became pregnant and for five months remained in seclusion. ²⁵ "The Lord has done this for me," she said. "In these days he has shown his favor and taken away my disgrace among the people."

The Birth of Jesus Foretold

²⁶ In the sixth month of Elizabeth's pregnancy, God sent the angel Gabriel to Nazareth, a town in Galilee, ²⁷ to a virgin pledged to be married to a man named Joseph, a descendant of David. The virgin's name was Mary. ²⁸ The angel went to her and said, "Greetings, you who are highly favored! The Lord is with you."

²⁹ Mary was greatly troubled at his words and wondered what kind of greeting this might be. ³⁰ But the angel said to her, "Do not be afraid, Mary; you have found favor with God. ³¹ You will conceive and give birth to a son, and you are to call him Jesus. ³² He will be great and will be called the Son of the Most High. The Lord God will give him the throne of his father David, ³³ and he will reign over Jacob's descendants forever; his kingdom will never end."

³⁴ "How will this be," Mary asked the angel, "since I am a virgin?"

35 The angel answered, "The Holy Spirit will come on you, and the power of the Most High will overshadow you. So the holy one to be born will be called[a] the Son of God. 36 Even Elizabeth your relative is going to have a child in her old age, and she who was said to be unable to conceive is in her sixth month. 37 For no word from God will ever fail."

38 "I am the Lord's servant," Mary answered. "May your word to me be fulfilled." Then the angel left her.

JOSEPH' STORY (MATTHEW 1:18-25)

Joseph Accepts Jesus as His Son

18 This is how the birth of Jesus the Messiah came about: His mother Mary was pledged to be married to Joseph, but before they came together, she was found to be pregnant through the Holy Spirit. 19 Because Joseph her husband was faithful to the law, and yet did not want to expose her to public disgrace, he had in mind to divorce her quietly.

20 But after he had considered this, an angel of the Lord appeared to him in a dream and said, "Joseph son of David, do not be afraid to take Mary home as your wife, because what is conceived in her is from the Holy Spirit. 21 She will give birth to a son, and you are to give him the name Jesus, because he will save his people from their sins."

22 All this took place to fulfill what the Lord had said through the prophet: 23 "The virgin will conceive and give birth to a son, and they will call him Immanuel." [The name Immanuel means "God with us," and this prophesy was made 600 years BC!]

24 When Joseph woke up, he did what the angel of the Lord had commanded him and took Mary home as his wife. 25 But he did not consummate their marriage until she gave birth to a son. And he gave him the name Jesus.

MARY'S STORY—PART II
(LUKE 1:39-45 AND LUKE 2:1-19)

Mary Visits Elizabeth

39 At that time Mary got ready and hurried to a town in the hill country of Judea, 40 where she entered Zechariah's home and greeted Elizabeth. 41 When Elizabeth heard Mary's greeting, the baby leaped in her womb, and Elizabeth was filled with the Holy Spirit. 42 In a loud voice she

exclaimed: "Blessed are you among women, and blessed is the child you will bear! ⁴³ But why am I so favored, that the mother of my Lord should come to me? ⁴⁴ As soon as the sound of your greeting reached my ears, the baby in my womb leaped for joy. ⁴⁵ Blessed is she who has believed that the Lord would fulfill his promises to her!"

The Birth of Jesus

2 In those days Caesar Augustus issued a decree that a census should be taken of the entire Roman world. 2 (This was the first census that took place while[a] Quirinius was governor of Syria.) ³ And everyone went to their own town to register.

⁴ So Joseph also went up from the town of Nazareth in Galilee to Judea, to Bethlehem the town of David, because he belonged to the house and line of David. ⁵ He went there to register with Mary, who was pledged to be married to him and was expecting a child. ⁶ While they were there, the time came for the baby to be born, ⁷ and she gave birth to her firstborn, a son. She wrapped him in cloths and placed him in a manger, because there was no guest room available for them.

⁸ And there were shepherds living out in the fields nearby, keeping watch over their flocks at night. ⁹ An angel of the Lord appeared to them, and the glory of the Lord shone around them, and they were terrified. ¹⁰ But the angel said to them, "Do not be afraid. I bring you good news that will cause great joy for all the people. ¹¹ Today in the town of David a Savior has been born to you; he is the Messiah, the Lord. ¹² This will be a sign to you: You will find a baby wrapped in cloths and lying in a manger."

¹³ Suddenly a great company of the heavenly host appeared with the angel, praising God and saying, ¹⁴ "Glory to God in the highest heaven, and on earth peace to those on whom his favor rests." ¹⁵ When the angels had left them and gone into heaven, the shepherds said to one another, "Let's go to Bethlehem and see this thing that has happened, which the Lord has told us about." ¹⁶ So they hurried off and found Mary and Joseph, and the baby, who was lying in the manger. ¹⁷ When they had seen him, they spread the word concerning what had been told them about this child, ¹⁸ and all who heard it were amazed at what the shepherds said to them. ¹⁹ But Mary treasured up all these things and pondered them in her heart.

AFTERWORD

THE ADVENT SEASON is over; another year is gone. Have you journeyed through the season unchanged?

The manger points to the Cross. The baby lying in the manger of Bethlehem was the Promised One introduced to Adam as the Deliverer of his sinful, lost, rebellious heart. On that starry night 2,000 years ago, God took the form of a man—the Anointed One. Jesus was anointed to do His Father's will before there was time or space.

He stepped down from the dwelling place of God as Immanuel, "God With Us." He was and is the only pure gift God had to give for the redemption of the human heart. His purpose was to come as the Messiah, the Savior, to die on the Cross of Calvary. His death and resurrection provided an escape from the sins that bind each of us and from an everlasting eternity in Hell.

With God's authority, the author of Romans 3:23 wrote that every person, at all times and in all places, has sinned and fallen short of God's holiness. He pointed out in Romans 6:23 that the punishment for our sinful heart is spiritual and physical death. Despite their wretchedness, Jesus told His disciples that He loved them with the same love His Father had for Him. Jesus loves us as He loved His disciples. He loves to a depth we cannot fathom. He loves across race, sex, and religion. He loved to extreme by shedding His blood on the Cross of Calvary to set man free from the punishment his wicked heart deserves. Man is a sinner doomed and self-condemned to be separated from God forever. Jesus' heart wrenches at the thought of any one of us being separated from Him in an eternal Hell.

He knew man was not capable of redeeming himself. The apostle Paul wrote in Ephesians 2:8-9, "8 For it is by grace you have been saved, through faith—and this is not from yourselves, it is the gift of God— 9 not by works, so that no one can boast." His love for man was so intense, He made a way to bring man to Himself.

Jesus died on the Cross as the Lamb of God. In John 3:16-18, Jesus said:

> 16For God so loved the world that he gave his one and only Son, that whoever believes in him shall not perish but have eternal life. 17For God did not send his Son into the world to condemn the world, but to save the world through him.

Jesus does not condemn us; we condemn ourselves by not accepting His great gift of salvation.

His gift would have been meaningless, and His death would have carried no power in our lives if His grave had not been empty. He would have been like all other fallen kings. He would have gone to the grave and stayed there, left a legacy for the country He ruled, and had His story written in history books. But Jesus was not like other kings; He arose from the dead by His own authority, which was given to Him by His Father (John 10:18). Stepping through the door of the tomb, He conquered sin, death, and hell.

Have you rambled through life, familiar with these words, perhaps even having read them, but never have truly understood truth? Jesus is including you today when he says that "…he is patient with you, not wanting anyone to perish, but everyone to come to repentance" (2 Peter 3:9).

The message for today's culture remains the same as when Jesus spoke during His earthly stay. His message compels people who are hurting, broken, tormented, feeling as though they are never enough, abandoned, unloved and unwanted, narcissistic, or feeling unworthy, to come to Him. Jesus proclaimed in the book of John, "I am the way and the truth and the life. No one comes to the Father except through me" (John 14:6).

Jesus is a gentleman whispering love into your heart when long nights haunt your soul with the day's sins. He is reaching out in grace and compassion, waiting for you to accept His great gift of Salvation. You have nothing you could possibly give to Him to merit His gift. He has given His all to you!

How can you open yourself to Him?

God states it simply so that we can understand His words:

> ⁹ If you declare with your mouth, "Jesus is Lord," and believe in your heart that God raised him from the dead, you will be saved. ¹⁰ For it is with your heart that you believe and are justified, and it is with your mouth that you profess your faith and are saved (Romans 10:9-10).

Jesus longs for you to accept His grace-gift of salvation. He wants that for you today. If you will allow Him to become your King, Jesus has this to say to you:

> …he who created you…he who formed you…"Do not fear, for I have redeemed you; I have summoned you by name; you are mine.
> For I am the LORD your God, the Holy One of Israel, your Savior; Since you are precious and honored in my sight, and because I love you… (Isaiah 43:1-4).

Changed lives are why His name carries a legacy that has withstood the changing philosophy of time! THE BABY OF BETHLEHEM IS THE KING OF KINGS AND LORD OF LORDS!

HISTORY OF THE ADVENT

The word "Advent" is translated as "Coming" in Latin and reflects the three-fold significance of the Advent Season.

First is the expectation and anticipation of the birth of Immanuel—God With Us. Micah, the Old Testament prophet, predicted a ruler "whose origins are of old, from ancient times" (Micah 5:2), would be born in the small, obscure town of Bethlehem. Throughout history foreign thrones ruled the Jewish people who anticipated and yearned for a ruler who could deliver them from tyrannical control. Although His rejection has spread through centuries and nations, Immanuel is the deliverer.

Second is the repentance that results in the transformation that takes place within the heart and mind of those who love the Baby and recognize Him as Savior. It requires looking inward, grasping the truth of a sinful heart, turning to Jesus, and acknowledging that He is the only way for redemption to take place.

Third is the hope of Jesus' return to Earth, a second time, when He will establish His Kingdom. He will come in majestic power and glory and reign from a Kingdom that will never end. In our upside-down, torn-apart world, we see Christ's return clearer than past generations. It is our hope, peace, and desire to see the King take His rightful place as Ruler of the Universe.

The origin of the Advent is questionable. There is limited proven evidence supporting the country or religion that gave birth to the observance. From early 301 A.D., history reveals multiple countries observed the Advent. However, there are sustaining manuscripts from 367 A.D. directing attention to Gaul, a territory in Western Europe which included France and inhabited by the Celts, as the framer of the first three-week preparation of Epiphany.

During the 5th century, writings acknowledge France participated in a 40-day fast beginning on St. Martin's Day and extending through Epiphany. St. Martin of Tours, the third bishop of Tours, was born in 316 A.D. He was known for his love and care of children and the poor. St. Martin's Day is November 11, the day of his funeral, not his death. January 6th is Epiphany which celebrates the feast of the wise men, most likely astrologers, as the Star of Bethlehem led them to the Christ Child. The purpose of a 40-day fast, sometimes called St. Martin's Lent, connected Christ's temptation in the wilderness with the temptation believers experience.

Leading into the 6th century, fasting (the Nativity Fast) became a way of celebrating the events of Christ's life and became an intricate part of the Christmas celebration. Fasting is a religious practice. Its purpose is a voluntary purging of the body from meat, dairy, grain, alcohol, or even activities that distract from aligning our heart with the love and desire of God. It is a discipline of living in total abandon to prayer and meditation on God's Word.

Fasting and devoting the first four Sundays before Christmas to the Christ Child and His birth spread throughout the known world.

Between the 10th and 14th centuries, fasting lost its purpose and faded from the practice of Advent. The 15th century gave birth to a new tradition with an old message. The custom moved from fasting to feasting.

In Germany, aspects of the Advent Season, including the wreath and tree, had its origin with Lutheran believers between the 15th and 16th centuries. Advent Season began on the fourth Sunday (St. Andrew's Day) before Christmas. St. Andrew was the brother of the Apostle Peter. The two men were fishermen by trade who made the decision to become disciples of Jesus.

In the 17th century, when religious reform took place in Europe, Oliver Cromwell canceled Christmas and any related practice, including Advent. He and his Puritan comrades took over

England in 1645 and purged the country of all its excessive indulgence, including Christmas. It was restored by Charles II when he was returned to the throne.

Abstinence from celebrating Christmas was enforced in America when the Pilgrims arrived in 1620. They had even stricter views than Cromwell and forbade the celebration. Boston actually outlawed Christmas from 1659-1681.

The next 150 years brought little or no change to the Advent tradition.

In 1839, the modern Advent wreath was introduced by Johann Hinrich Wichern, a German Protestant pastor. As Europe became more influential in American culture, so did the Advent wreath. Over the years, the holiday gradually grew in popularity until Christmas was made a national holiday in America on June 6, 1870, restoring the Advent tradition. The Advent wreath became a desired practice in Orthodox churches.

Over the last 60 years, the Advent has not only become a religious practice, but it has also evolved into a family event of peace and quiet moments during the holidays. It is an act of worship honoring the birth of The King—Jesus.

REFERENCES

DEVOTIONAL ONE

Wikipedia The Free Encyclopedia, (2020, July 4) Come, Thou Long Expected Jesus https://en.wikipedia.org/wiki/Come,_Thou_Long_Expected_Jesus accessed 2020, July 24

Zachary Houghton, (2017, December 13) Behind the Hymn: Come, Thou Long-Expected Jesus. http://www.restoration.community/blog/2017/12/13/behind-the-hymn-come-thou-long-expected-jesus

Chris Fenner for Hymnology Archive, (29 May 2019) Come, Thou Long Expected Jesus. https://www.hymnologyarchive.com/come-thou-long-expected-jesus

BBC, Religions, (2009, August 6) Charles Wesley

https://www.bbc.co.uk/religion/religions/christianity/people/charleswesley_1.shtml

Merriam-Webster since 1828, (2020 July 23) Prediction Merriam-Webster.com Dictionary, Merriam-Webster, https://www.merriam-webster.com/dictionary/prediction. https://www.merriam-webster.com/dictionary/prediction accessed 2020, July 24

Merriam-Webster since 1828, (2020 July 4) Prophecy Merriam-Webster.com Dictionary, Merriam-Webster, https://www.merriam-webster.com/dictionary/prophecy. accessed 2020, July 24

DEVOTIONAL TWO

Josh McDowell and Bob Hostetler, (1994) Right from Wrong (Nashville Tennessee: Word Publishing), 17.

Technology.org, (2018, December 22) 7 Interesting Facts about snow – what it is, what's its colour and how warm are igloos? https://www.technology.org/2018/12/22/7-interesting-facts-about-snow-what-it-is-whats-its-colour-and-how-warm-are-igloos/ (Please use your browser to look up this article.)

Johnathan Belles, The Weather Channel An IMB Business, (2016, November 6) 10 Facts About Snow That Might Surprise You. https://weather.com/science/weather-explainers/news/ten-factsabouthow?cm_ven=PS_GGL_DSA_09162019_1&par=MK_GGL&gclid=Cj0KCQjwyPbzBRDsARIsAFh15JbwMgKbpV5B-MtG0eVNZTCxGMpIHYVV1d4GfqMEZCQ2-5uqmgxTRAssaAgvoEALw_wcBWO accessed 2020, February 10

Wikipedia The Free Encyclopedia (2020, July 15) Spectralon

https://en.wikipedia.org/wiki/Spectralon accessed 2020, July 20

Interesting Engineering, (n.d) https://interestingengineering.com/video/youtuber-shines-a-high-powered-laser-on-whitest-white-and-blackest-black YouTube

Wikipedia The Free Encyclopedia, (2020, May 22) O Holy Night

https://en.wikipedia.org/wiki/O_Holy_Night

Douglas D. Anderson, (n.d.) Hymns and Carols of Christmas

http://www.hymnsandcarolsofchristmas.com/Hymns_and_Carols/o_holy_night.htm

James M. Boice, (1983 & 2009). The Christ of Christmas. (Phillipsburg: New Jersey, P&R Publishing)

DEVOTIONAL THREE

Musicnotes Sheet Music Anywhere, (n.d.) Written in Red

https://www.musicnotes.com/sheetmusic/mtd.asp?ppn=mn0155911

Silent Night Association, (n.d.) History of the Song

Bill Egan, (2005, November 21) Powerful Message of Heavenly Peace

https://www.stillenacht.at/en/history-of-the-song

Douglas Anderson, (n.d.) The Hymns and Carols of Christmas

http://www.hymnsandcarolsofchristmas.com/Hymns_and_Carols/Notes_On_Carols/silent_night_holy_night_notes.htm

WebCite, Mag.Manfred W.K. Fuscger & Renate Schaffenberger

https://www.webcitation.org/6Dy0uz8v3?url=http://www.stillenacht.at/en/mohr.asp

The German Way & More, (n.d.) Stille Nacht/Silent Night – The True Story https://www.german-way.com/history-and-culture/holidays-and-celebrations/christmas/stille-nacht-silent-night/

James M. Boice, (1983 & 2009) The Christ of Christmas. (Phillipsburg, New Jersey: P&R Publishing), 21-23.

A – The National Archives, (2020) British Battles, From Crimea to Korea https://www.nationalarchives.gov.uk/battles/crimea/

Henry Allen Ironside, (1975) Illustrations of Bible Truth. (Addison, Illinois: Bible Truth Publishers), 131

DEVOTIONAL FOUR

Jill Carattini RAIM, (n.d.) Lamb of God https://www.rzim.org/read/a-slice-of-infinity/lamb-of-god

David Guzik, (2014) The Word and the Witness

https://www.blueletterbible.org/Comm/guzik_david/StudyGuide2017-Jhn/Jhn-1.cfm?a=998029

David Guzik, (2012) Philip and the Samaritans https://www.blueletterbible.org/Comm/guzik_david/StudyGuide2017-Act/Act-8.cfm

Caroline Picard, (2019, May 6) 30 Royal Baby Traditions You Didn't Realize Existed https://www.goodhousekeeping.com/life/parenting/g5096/royal-family-baby-traditions/

Douglas D. Anderson, The Hymns and Carols of Christmas (2014, April 28) http://www.hymnsandcarolsofchristmas.com/Hymns_and_Carols/o_little_town_of_bethlehem.htm

Connie Ruth Christiansen, O Little Town of Bethlehem, the Song and Story https://www.sharefaith.com/guide/Christian-Holidays/holiday-songs/o-little-town-of-bethlehem,-the-song-and-the-story.html

Pat Higgins, What the Bible says about God's Love for Christ (From Forerunner Commentary)

https://www.bibletools.org/index.cfm/fuseaction/topical.show/RTD/cgg/ID/2638/Gods-Love-for-Christ.htm

Melody Chapman, (1991), A Decorated Box, Pittsburgh, California

DEVOTIONAL FIVE

Douglas D. Anderson, The Hymns and Carols of Christmas, (2014, April 28)

http://www.hymnsandcarolsofchristmas.com/Hymns_and_Carols/joy_to_the_world-1.htm

Wikipedia The Free Encyclopedia, (2020, April 24) Isaac Watts

https://en.wikipedia.org/wiki/Isaac_Watts

Wikipedia The Free Encyclopedia, (2020, July 25) Lion https://en.wikipedia.org/wiki/Lion accessed 2020, July, 25

Smithsonian's National Zoo & Conservation Biology Institute, Great Cats-Lion https://nationalzoo.si.edu/animals/lion

National Geographic, Animals-African Lion https://www.nationalgeographic.com/animals/mammals/a/african-lion/

HISTORY OF THE ADVENT

Wikipedia The Free Encyclopedia, (2020, June 6) Advent https://en.wikipedia.org/wiki/Advent accessed 2020, July 24

Wikipedia The Free Encyclopedia, (2020, July 21) St. Martin's Day

https://en.wikipedia.org/wiki/St._Martin%27s_Day accessed 2020, July 24

Wikipedia The Free Encyclopedia, (2020, June 9) Saint Andrew's Day https://en.wikipedia.org/wiki/Saint_Andrew%27s_Day accessed 2020, July 24

History of Christmas, (2020, January 27, Original Published Date 2009, October 27) History of Christmas https://www.history.com/topics/christmas/history-of-christmas

DEVOTIONAL FIVE

Herbert Lockyer, All the Messianic Prophecies of the Bible (Grand Rapids, Michigan: Zondervan, 1973), 69

IMAGES

DEVOTIONAL ONE

Image #1

Marty Jones, (2017, November) The Prophet Isaiah, 2017, November 16

www.mjarts.com

Attribution: Marty Jones

Purchased by Linda Fields under contract. All rights reserved.

Image #2

Charles Wesley & Christian Friedrich Witt, (2018, March 25) https://en.wikipedia.org/wiki/Come,_Thou_Long_Expected_Jesus from The Hymnal: as authorized and approved by the General Convention of the Protestant Episcopal Church in the United States of America in the year of our Lord 1916

https://commons.wikimedia.org/wiki/File:Come,_Thou_long-expected_Jesus.jpg

FILE URL http://www.hymnary.org/hymn/EH1916/55 Attribution Charles Wesley, Christian Friedrich Witt, Public Domain

Image #3

Charles Wesley (2017, February 19)

Page URL: https://commons.wikimedia.org/wiki/File:Charles_Wesley.jpg

File URL: https://upload.wikimedia.org/wikipedia/commons/e/e2/Charles_Wesley.jpg

Attribution: User Magnus Manske on en.wikipedia / Public domain

Image #4

MarywithDonkeyonthewaytoBethlehem,

https://www.istockphoto.com/photo/joseph-and-mary-with-donkey- on the-way-to-bethlehem=gm499184232-800765057st=p_80076505

Attribution: Mastapiece

DEVOTIONAL TWO

Image #5

Holy Night with Angles and Shepherds

http://www.thinkstock.com/angels-andshepherd=497838722

Attribution: Mastapiece

Image #6

Song – O Holy Night, Linda Fields

Image #7

Placide Cappeau – (2020, June 11)

Page URL: https://commons.wikimedia.org/wiki/File:Placide_Cappeau.jpg

File URL: https://upload.wikimedia.org/wikipedia/commons/e/ed/Placide_Cappeau.jpg

Attribution: Unknown middle XIXe / Public domain

Image #8

Girls Sitting By Window and Looking at Santa (2016, November 09)

https://www.canstockphoto.com/girls-sitting-by-window-and-looking-at-41693853.html

Attribution: Choreograph

DEVOTIONAL THREE

Image #9

The Cradle and the Cross

https://www.thinkstockphoto.com/photo/empty-manger-with-cross-shadow-gm499512706-80269487

Attribution: Ginosphotos

Image #10

Song – Silent Night –

Page URL: https://commons.wikimedia.org/wiki/File:Sheaves_of_song_(IA_sheavesofsong00mcco).pdf

File URL: https://upload.wikimedia.org/wikipedia/commons/8/87/Sheaves_of_song_%28IA_sheavesofsong00mcco%29.pdf

Attribution: [McConnell, Marion Delana Daniel] [from old catalog] / Public domain

Image #11

Josef Mohr, (2014, December 24)

PAGE URL: https://commons.wikimedia.org/wiki/File:Joseph_Hermann_Mohr.jpeg

FILE URL: https://upload.wikimedia.org/wikipedia/commons/7/77/Joseph_Hermann_Mohr.jpeg

Attribution: Unknown author / Public domain

Image #12

Celebration Theme with Christmas Gifts (2012, October 26)

https://www.canstockphoto.com/celebration-theme-with-christmas-gifts-11306555.html

Attribution: Jag_cz

DEVOTIONAL FOUR

Image #13

Madonna and Child Nativity (2008, August 08)

https://www.canstockphoto.com/madonna-and-child-nativity-15243870.html

Attribution: Irisangel

Image #14

Phillips Brooks, A Sketch by His Private Secretary

PageURL: https://commons.wikimedia.org/wiki/File:A_sketch_of_the_late_Rt._Rev._Phillips_Brooks,_D.D._(IA_sketchoflatertre00broo).pdf

File URL: https://commons.wikimedia.org/wiki/File:A_sketch_of_the_late_Rt._Rev._Phillips_Brooks,_D.D._(IA_sketchoflatertre00broo).pdf

Attribution: Brooks, William Henry, 1846- / Public domain

Song – O Little Town of Bethlehem – Linda Fields

Image #15

Phillip Brooks (2016, February 9)

Page URL: https://commons.wikimedia.org/wiki/File:Life_and_letters_of_Phillips_Brooks_(1900)_(148018373230.jpg

FILE URL: https://upload.wikimedia.org/wikipedia/commons/f/f1/Life_and_letters_of_Phillips_Brooks_%281900%29_%2814801837323%29.jpg

Attribution: Internet Archive Book Images / No restrictions

Image #16

Christmas lights seen through a Wooden Cabin Window, (2014, November 08)

https://www.istockphoto.com/photo/christmas-lights-seen-through-a-wooden-cabin-window-gm522359633-50753460

Attribution: Credit: alga38

DEVOTIONAL FIVE

Image #17

Marty Jones, (2017, November) The Victorious King

www.mjarts.com

Attribution: Marty Jones

Image #18

Song- Joy to the World

Page URL: https://commons.wikimedia.org/wiki/File:Joy_To_The_World_in_Bulgarian_by_Stoian_Vatlarski,_music_-_H%C3%A4ndel.jpg

File URL: https://upload.wikimedia.org/wikipedia/commons/d/d5/Joy_To_The_World_in_Bulgarian_by_Stoian_Vatlarski%2C_music_-_H%C3%A4ndel.jpg

Attribution: Стоян Ватларски(Life time: Mar 7 1860 - Aug 30 1935) / Public domain

Image #19

Isaac Watts, (2020, May 13)

PAGE URL: https://commons.wikimedia.org/wiki/File:Isaac_Watts_from_NPG.jpg

FILE URL: https://upload.wikimedia.org/wikipedia/commons/9/9d/Isaac_Watts_from_NPG.jpg

Attribution: National Portrait Gallery / Public domain

Image #20

God of the Bible, Lion of Judah (2015, October 6)

https://www.istockphoto.com/photo/god-of-the-bible-lion-of-judah-gm48541315738655828

Attribution: ninjaMonkeyStudio

ALL CHAPTERS

Christmas Musical Card, Treble Clef and Fir Trees Silver Glitter, (2011, February 9

https://www.canstockphoto.com/christmas-musical-card-treble-clef-and-74615295.html

Attribution: LABE

Made in United States
Orlando, FL
27 November 2021